DIRTY TRICK

MICKEY MILLER

To Rhonda,
Enjoy this bad boy :)

I, Mickey Miller

Edited by
CARLY BORNSTEIN-HAYWARD

Edited by
NANCY SMAY

PROLOGUE

The Daily Grind Prison Gossip Column

Folsom Prison - California

A small crowd gathered outside in the rain last night to watch famed billionaire, and alleged top drug dealer in the Southern California area, Corbin Young, as he was let out of prison after just two years for "Good Behavior."

Corbin Young is rumored to be the mastermind behind billions of dollars in flow of drugs across the border over the past decade. Although authorities were unable to prove him the "source" and instead charged him as a lower level dealer.

At the time of the trial, Corbin garnered national coverage for several reasons. Not the least of which was the viral hashtag #Idbuyfromhim, which swiffered the nation along with a shirtless pic of Mr. Young, now twenty-nine years old.

His reckless disregard for the law seemed a boon, not a challenge, when it came to the ladies for Mr. Young.

The circumstances of his release are still under investigation, as some believed he should have never been let out of prison.

Corbin Young declined to comment for this interview.

1

EVA

Tijuana, Mexico: 9:34 p.m. on a Saturday

HE WAS EXACTLY the kind of guy my mother warned me about.

And I kissed him anyway.

Well, more than kiss.

Let's back up though. Let me tell this story from the beginning.

Honestly, I didn't even want to go out that night, but Amanda insisted we do something fun. Personally, I'd always thought birthdays were overrated.

But now we were two good girls in Tijuana looking for trouble.

At least I'd always considered myself a good girl. But there was something in the air that made me feel like I might be just a teensy bit bad. Maybe it was turning twenty-seven. Or maybe it was because I'd just gotten out of a lengthy failed relationship.

Little did I know just how bad I could get.

The music pulsed inside the club through the hot Mexico air as we waited in line.

"This is one of those nights where if something seems like a great decision at the time, we should just go for it. Live a little," my friend Amanda said as she tossed her hair. "Because as we all know, what happens in Tijuana stays in Tijuana."

"Doesn't the DEA have undercover agents everywhere?" I countered. "What if they see me dancing like a fool?"

"Oh is it against the law to have a good night of dancing? Please. Don't be ridiculous."

For the last three years, I'd barely sparsely attended a party. I was too busy working days at the DEA and laboring nights finishing my Ph.D. in criminal justice. I was paranoid by nature, and the fact that one of my coworkers just had a viral drinking meme made about her made me extra weary about truly letting loose tonight.

Amanda gave me an 'are you seriously still talking about work' shrug and flashed me a mischievous grin as she handed her passport to the bouncer. I was a little shocked that this shady Tijuana club was even checking IDs, but I passed mine over as well.

Inside, sweaty bodies pulsed around us, men and women dancing to the beat of the reggaeton. The seedy club was the type of place Amanda and I *expected* to get a drink spilled on us. Which is why we'd planned ahead and bought inexpensive—but still hot—outfits for the occasion. Mine was a red, tight fitted bodycon number I found rummaging in a sale bin. The stunner was Amanda's black, scoop neck, high-waisted skirt and crop top that complimented her curvy figure.

We were looking for a good time, not a high-end club serving twenty-dollar cocktails, so this place was perfect. I settled against the sticky bar to scope out the terrain. Over the screaming speakers bleeding Latino salsa, somehow the problems I was having with relationships and my job back in San Diego faded away, if only momentarily.

"You know Eva, I'm glad you two broke up. Really, I am," Amanda smiled, tossing her blond locks in an attempt to get the bartender's attention. "He wasn't that great anyway. I always thought he was a little shady."

I turned to look at her, but my dress didn't turn with me —it was stuck to the bar. *Gross.*

"Shady is an understatement," I emphasized. As much as I wanted to, I couldn't tell Amanda the whole truth about why I'd broken up with my boyfriend. It was something I was still dealing with. And if I couldn't handle the truth myself, why would I expect she'd be able to?

In college at San Diego State, Amanda and I both majored in Psychology. She knew my dating habits better than I did. I'd always heeded my foster mom's advice, and she'd told me to stay away from the bad guys, the unreliable guys. The guys who were apt to leave you high and dry.

Guys like my birth father, a man I'd never met.

I glanced across the bar, trying to figure out why we were still without drinks, when I glimpsed an extremely attractive man, tall and tattooed.

A chill went through my body from head to toe, and I wasn't sure if it was the good or the bad kind.

The man looked like he might be the type of criminal I might have chased down at my day job.

Except behind the tattoos and slightly evil smirk, there was a clear handsomeness about this one.

My stare lingered on him as he spoke with the bartender, a cocky grin spread across his face the entire time. His broad shoulders and thick biceps were covered with a white V-neck. The tight shirt accentuated each muscle, while tattoos poked out of the neckline and covered his arms. His irises were an icey blue hue, and when he ran a hand over his short brown hair I had to bite my lip. More than a few days of stubble covered his face.

His gaze shifted, our eyes locked, and he didn't look away. I didn't either, frozen by the man's gorgeous face.

He seemed like a guy who could probably get any girl he wanted, and *would* leave her high and dry given the chance. Still, a current of electricity ignited inside me.

Finally I averted my gaze, his cocky grin seared into my brain. A faint dizzy flutter rolled through my chest, spread to my fingertips, and reached my toes. It was like morphine spreading through my limbs.

I stole one more glance at him out of the corner of my eye. Two gorgeous girls were clawing at each other to position themselves closer to him, but he just appeared bored.

Used to their attention.

He nodded at the bartender and eyeballed a bottle of mezcal behind the bar. Almost instantly he had four shots of the liquid in front of him. After he took his drink, he put his shot glass down, looked right at me again, and leered with a smirk like he was thinking of some funny joke I hadn't figured out yet.

"Hey, buddy!" Amanda yelled to the bartender, before turning to me. Still, he ignored Amanda. "Geez! The bartender must be talking to his best friend or something.

It's like we're ghosts. Do I not have the twins out tonight? I'm starting to feel insecure."

I looked down at Amanda's top. Usually we got quick service. "The twins are definitely ready to play tonight. Maybe the bartender is gay?" I joked.

She rolled her eyes and sighed. And I turned away from the bar in an effort not to stare at Mr. Sexy Eyes. In the process, I accidently made eye contact with an out of shape, fortyish man with thinning black hair and a mustache, who smiled back at me. I cringed, immediately spinning back around and tapping Amanda on the shoulder.

"Creepy guy coming, five o'clock. We need to change locations, stat," I warned.

We spun around to look for another opening at the bar, but it was too late. Mr. Mustache moved quickly so he was right next to us, boxing us in. Up close, he was even less attractive than he had been when he was ten feet away.

"Well hello, *amor,*" he said over the music. "How about I buy you a drink?"

Amor, really?

"I'm not anyone's *amor,*" I said simply, hoping he'd take the hint.

I glanced over at the tall man with the tattoos again. He was ordering more shots.

Damn, the man could drink.

Lifting his chin, he winked at me as he took them from the bartender. Well at least if we weren't getting service, someone was.

The mustached man didn't budge, not taking the hint that we wanted him gone. Instead of leaving us alone, he moved closer.

"Oh well if you don't have an *amor,* I can be your *amor*

tonight. Do you want to split a beer?" he offered, opening his wallet.

"Split a beer? Is that a thing?" Amanda shot back.

"My funds are low tonight," the man continued patting his wallet. "So we have to split just one. Don't you like beer?"

"No, we're fine," I responded tersely. I looked back to where the sexy beast with the tattoos had been standing, but he was gone.

My heart sank just a little bit. I wondered if he'd left.

"You don't have drinks yet, though," he pointed out, refusing to throw in the towel.

I shot Amanda a look. Apparently the twins were working, they just weren't attracting the right guy tonight.

"Uh, my boyfriend is here," I blurted out, trying not to sound too much like a liar.

"Yeah," Amanda said. "Both of our boyfriends are here."

The ugly man didn't budge. "No they aren't. You're lying. *Mentiras.* You said you don't have an *amor.* Please, just drink a beer with me. Come on, just one."

I eyed Amanda and tried to move away from the bar. Talking to creepy old men was exactly the opposite of how we wanted to spend my birthday.

Before I heard him, I swear I could sense him.

"Hey *honey,*" a man's low voice crooned from behind me.

I whipped around to see the tattooed hottie right behind us holding three shots in one big hand, a relaxed grin plastered across his face. In a natural manner, he extended his free hand toward my shoulder and gave it a light squeeze, as if we were indeed boyfriend-girlfriend, and we'd done this a million times. A tingle ran down my spine when he touched me.

"I finally got those shots. Sorry it took so long, baby," he said in a deep and scratchy voice. He handed Amanda and I each a shot with a big smile on his face.

"Thank you, *baby*," I smiled, very willing to play his game for a moment in order to stave off Mr. Mustache's advances.

Although to be honest, I would play fake boyfriend and girlfriend with this man even if there wasn't a creepy old man hitting on me.

We clinked glasses and each threw back our shots. Still, the annoying man didn't leave.

"You two aren't together," the mustached man said. "I saw you girls walk in alone. And you—you've been with them all night." He pointed to the two girls who were standing a few feet away, eyeballing Amanda and me.

"Honey, let's make sure this man knows who you belong to," he growled, grinning.

Before I had a chance to react, Mr. Tattoos gripped the back of my head and crushed his lips to mine, making out with me.

He smelled like tequila and man and...*fucking sexy.*

I wrapped my arms around him as my heart beat like crazy. This wasn't a middle school first kiss. This hot, cocky stranger knew what he was doing.

"Ahem," I heard Amanda say.

When I opened my eyes and came back to earth, I saw the mustached man was gone.

The man's huge hand held onto my side.

I was getting so turned on already, after under a minute of touching him and barely even a word exchanged between us, and he'd turned me on even more than my last boyfriend had in two years of dating.

And I didn't even know his name.

Whoops, did I just admit that?

This kind of strong reaction was not normal for me.

My conscience kicked in and I realized as hot as this man was, he was one-hundred and ten percent *trouble*.

When my mom told me to stay away from men, I'm pretty sure this guy's picture was the one she used as a reference.

"Listen," I said, putting my hand on the man's shoulder. He was noticeably taller than me, and even in heels I had to angle my head up to address him. "Thanks for saving me from that creepy guy, but I don't go around kissing random guys whose names I don't even know. It's just not my thing."

"I'm Corbin." He stuck out a hand to shake mine. "Now you know me. Problem solved."

He was even more gorgeous up close. His lips curled up in a smirk that simultaneously scared and attracted me. The hairs on the back of my neck stood up and my fingertips burned as I touched his skin.

"Well, *Corbin*, I've dated guys like you. You're not my type, trust me."

"So you don't like guys who are hot, tall, and tattooed?" he quipped back. "Maybe I'll just have to show you what these big hands can do."

Without taking his eyes off me, he pressed his hands up against mine to do a quick comparison.

They were huge.

I tried to say something to him, but nothing came out.

"Beers! Who wants a Corona?" Amanda thankfully interrupted, handing each of us a cold bottle with a lime.

"You finally got through to the bartender," I said.

"Yeah. And the bartender told me these are on the house. He wouldn't accept payment for them. Said my money is no good when we're hanging out with...*you*."

Amanda tipped her forehead in Corbin's direction. "Are you like the Godfather or something?"

Corbin shrugged. "I have friends in low places. Or high ones, depending on how you look at it."

"What does that mean?" Amanda asked.

"Don't worry about it," Corbin said. "Just enjoy the ride. Cheers."

We clinked beers and all took a sip. My body tingled all over as I took the drink. And I wasn't sure if it was from my buzz, or from Corbin.

"So you know my name. But what are *your* names?" Corbin asked. "You never told me."

"My name is..." I paused and cleared my throat. I thought about what Amanda had said earlier. *What happens in Tijuana stays in Tijuana.*

Back home, I was the most responsible one of all of my friends. I'd studied harder, rarely partied, and worked my way through school and work the old fashioned way. Maybe it was the slight buzz from the tequila. Or maybe it was the existential crisis I was having on my twenty-seventh birthday.

But I decided I would not give this beautiful stranger my real name tonight.

"You okay?" Corbin asked, furrowing his brow while I thought in silence. I feigned like my beer had gone down the wrong pipe to buy some time.

I wasn't a liar. Screw it. Tonight--I wouldn't play the good girl.

I would be whoever I wanted to be.

"My name's Alexa," I lied.

As soon as the name came out, I shot Amanda that subtle look only best friends of years can give each other.

She didn't miss a beat.

"And I'm *Bambi*," she smiled broadly, and I swear her voice even took on this new, "bambi-like" quality.

I stifled a laugh, twirling my hair.

"Well, nice to meet you two. Listen, you've got to be careful in a place like this. You never know who you might meet." He paused, glancing across the bar. "Shit, my buddy is calling me from over on the other side of the bar. We're kind of having a...party."

"What are you celebrating?" I asked.

"Don't worry about it," he winked, and started in the direction of his friend.

Corbin might as well have had a warning sign on him that read: *Do not touch: Magnetic.* I reached my hand out and wrapped it around his forearm.

For some reason, the lie that I was "Alexa" made me feel powerful. Like instead of being this man's prey, I could transform into a predator.

She Wolf by Shakira came on. An omen.

"Are you sure you don't want to hang around for one more drink?" I asked, the words coming out a little throaty. My heart picked up its pace. Amanda shot me a subtle glance that gave me the impression she was wondering the same thing I was.

Where was this bold, flirty side of me coming from?

Corbin hesitated. "I would love to."

2

EVA

I've never told a lie.

Okay-that's probably an exaggeration.

But I've never outright pretended to be someone I'm not. Until tonight--and I realized I could do whatever I wanted, and when I walked into work next Monday, there would be no consequences.

"Why don't I invite my brother to hang out with us?" Corbin suggested.

"Is he as hot as you?" Amanda asked.

"I don't know Bambi, you tell me."

Corbin made a come-hither hand motion to a tall man standing several feet away. The man's lean build and bulging arms might have even been bigger than Corbin's. He had blond hair and one pierced eyebrow. As he strode toward us, Amanda blushed. He stopped right in front of her, extending his hand. "I'm Casey. Who might you two lovely ladies be?"

Smart. Corbin brought his brother as a wingman. Casey gave the impression that he might be a surfer one day and a Mafioso the next.

We introduced ourselves and a few minutes later, Casey swooped Amanda away for a quick smoke. She didn't protest, giving me a thumbs-up as they went.

"Where are you from?" I asked him.

"Southern California. You?"

"Originally from Chicago. But San Diego's been my home for years, since I went to San Diego State."

"Cool. You have brothers? Sisters?"

I balked at that question, which I never really knew how to answer. My biological father had a plethora of kids, but I didn't know most of them. And I didn't like bringing up who my brother was--since once guys knew I was Jake Napleton's sister--the best pitcher in the major leagues-- they mostly started asking me a bunch of baseball questions.

"I'm an only child," I lied again. "You?"

"One sister and one brother." He took a long pull of his beer, and I wondered what he was thinking about behind those eyes.

A man bumped into me, and I knocked forward, my chest landing in Corbin's.

It was like getting pushed into solid rock. Out of instinct, I placed my hand on his stomach, and my God did the man have abs you could wash clothes over.

I lingered for a moment longer than I needed if I were just catching my balance.

The song *Gasolina* played in the background, and I decided I'd keep up with my persona and have some fun tonight. Corbin's huge hand rested on my hips, and when I looked up at him he brought his lips down to mine to try and kiss me.

I dodged his advance, putting my finger over his lips.

I was going to make him work for it.

Spinning around, the music took me over. I ground my hips and ass into him, wiggling to the beat.

"Holy fuck, Alexa," he growled as he set his beer down and took me by the hips.

"Let's go," he said, and led me out to the dance floor.

Corbin was big but he could move.

For the next hour, I did something I'd been needing for months. Maybe *years*.

I let go.

I didn't dance like the responsible, hard working office student or office worker everyone knew me as.

I danced like I was a whole different person. Because I was, in a way.

I even saw Amanda's jaw wide open as she and Casey watched us from the edge of the dance floor. I loved the way Corbin's body felt rubbing up against mine. And, *damn*, I thought I felt something else below the belt, too.

An hour of reggaeton later, we exited the dance floor and headed back to the bar to rest.

"I can get this next round," I offered.

"Don't worry about it. I've got it."

Corbin waved his hand and in a few seconds, we had two more Coronas in front of us.

"Here you are Corbin," the bartender said. "It's just so nice to have you back."

I furrowed my brow, needing to get some answers. Everything Corbin said seemed so veiled, like he was hiding a big secret.

"Have you back? Where have you been?" I asked Corbin as we clinked bottles.

"Can I be honest with you?" he asked, and then took a swig of his beer.

"Of course."

"I'm a very forward person. And," he leaned his head down and pushed a lock of my hair behind my ear. "You, Alexa, are fucking gorgeous. This is me being one hundred percent honest."

I swallowed, and thanked him silently for reminding me that I'd given myself a fake name tonight.

I kept forgetting I was *not* Eva tonight.

I also considered for a moment that he had dodged my question. But staring into his river-blue eyes, I didn't really care who he was or where he'd been. The electrifying current running through me told me all I needed to know.

A COUPLE of hours later the music stopped, the club lights turned on and we headed outside. Amanda had danced the night away with Casey, and asked me if it was all right if she headed back to his place.

It wasn't Amanda or my usual move to go home with a guy after one night. Apparently, something was in the water tonight.

Or in the Coronas, more likely.

Corbin offered to take me back to the hotel room I'd rented--on his motorcycle. I got on behind him and gripped his muscled body, my arms wrapped around him as we flew against the warm night air.

We pulled up in front of my hotel on his motorcycle. Corbin turned and smiled at me, his strong jawline visible in the shadow of the street lamp. "So, you mind if I come up for one more?" he baited.

I pressed my hand to my heart, which thumped hard as I spoke the words. "Yes. I'd like that."

Inside the hotel room, I popped a mini bottle of vodka

and coke and poured some into a couple of glasses as we sat on the bed.

Corbin grinned and let his gaze linger on me, giving me the same deep stare that entranced me hours ago when we met. "Quite delicious." He swirled the liquid at eye level a few feet from my face, shooting me a look.

I scrunched my brow and took a sip. "Yeah, I agree it's not bad."

Corbin put his hand on my neck like he did the first time he'd touched me in the bar. "I wasn't talking about the wine. I was talking about *you,* Alexa. You look *delicious."*

Softly, he ran his lips over the nape of my neck. I leaned my head back as he worked slow kisses, threading my fingers through his thick hair.

Holy shit.

This was happening.

Who was this happening to, Eva or Alexa?

I didn't know, but I liked it.

He wrapped kisses in a U-shape down from my neck, close to my breasts, and back up the other side. My skin tingled, making me even more sensitive to his touch.

For a moment, he pulled his lips back, away from me.

"How does that feel?" he murmured.

"Good," I smiled, almost shyly. "You're good at that. Really good."

"Thanks," he smiled. "And you..."

He ran a hand along my bare arm as his eyes examined me from head to toe.

"Me what?" I asked.

"You...are fucking gorgeous."

"Oh," I mewled, blood rushing to my face.

"I've been thinking about doing this since the moment I

saw you in the bar." When he spoke, every word seemed deliberate and confident.

"Doing what exactly?" I asked.

"Better if I show you."

He pulled me gently to my feet before he pinned me against the wall. I breathed deeply as our chests pressed together, his lips devouring me. Reaching a hand under his shirt, my fingers ran over his rock hard abs.

Seriously. Was this guy a professional fighter or something? No one's abs should be that hard.

As our bodies grinded together my dress rode up my legs, exposing my panties. I let out a slight moan as we made out for what seemed like hours, but could have been minutes.

I felt his length gradually growing beneath his jeans.

"Oh hello," I said. "And wow."

"He says hello, too," Corbin smiled.

He brought his mouth to mine, parting my lips with his tongue. I let out a soft moan and dug my fingernails into his back through the cloth of his shirt. Corbin took off his shirt and I ran my hand over his abs. Through his pants, I could feel his length graze my leg. He let out a low growl.

"Jesus you're sexy," he grinned as he gripped the bottom of my dress and rolled it up. I helped him slip it up over my head. He lifted me up by the hips with seemingly little effort.

We made out for a few minutes like that before he set me on my back.

"Oh God," I moaned. "Yes."

He devoured my lips again, and found my clit through my black thong, moving his finger in a gentle circle. Our foreheads touched and we gazed into each other's eyes. Breaking eye contact, he began to work his mouth down my body. Starting at my neck, he slipped my bra off like an expert and kissed my breasts, down to my stomach, until he reached the lace of my thong. Corbin pulled at it with his teeth. I lifted my hips and he slipped it off.

"How bad do you want this," he teased in a low voice, and tossing the thong to the ground.

"Shut up and go down on me," I said, surprising even myself at how forceful the words sounded coming out.

Softly, he worked his tongue along my inner thigh until he was inches from my clit.

Slowly, tantalizingly, he brought his mouth to my other leg toward my calf.

"Please Corbin. Just...stop teasing me," I begged.

I wanted him to touch me. *Now.*

Finally his tongue reached my clit. I tingled with pleasure while he flicked it softly.

"Yes," I moaned.

The man definitely knows what he's doing down there.

His hands touched my chin and nodded forward to view him. He dipped the tip of his finger in my mouth. I wrapped my lips around it as he worked me, my hips gyrating in sync with his strokes.

Finally, Corbin released me from his grip and stood up next to the bed. I propped myself up on my elbow while he slipped his jeans and boxers off, revealing another tattoo around his midsection. From there my gaze drifted downward.

"I know it's big, thanks," Corbin ran his hand over the tattoo on his stomach, speaking in a low voice. "When I decided I wanted tattoos, I wasn't going to get some tiny little tat. Go big or go home, that's always been my motto."

"Oh, right," I say sarcastically. "Well it *is* big."

Because I was definitely thinking about how big your tattoo was and not the size of anything else.

I stared at Corbin for one more beat. Following my gaze, he grabbed his length, stroking it as his eyes fell on me.

"Alexa, are you ready for this?" he asked, smirking.

"Who is Alexa?" I reflexively asked, and scrunched my face, confused. As soon as the words came out, I covered my mouth and my heart dropped to my knees.

I remembered: *Oh right. I'm Alexa.*

Corbin squinted at me. "I can't tell if you're fucking with me right now." He leaned in and whispered in my ear. "And I kind of *like* it."

"Yeah I am! Did I almost have you?" I smiled, hoping Corbin wouldn't notice anything was amiss.

I was too deep into my fake persona to stop now.

"Well, *Alexa,*" he said, emphasizing each syllable, "are you ready for this? Are you...shit. I don't have any condoms."

I glanced between his legs at his length one more time. "I'm ready," I hummed, nodding at him. "I'm on the pill."

"Okay." He reached to a lock of my hair, tucking it behind my ear. "Ready for what? Tell me you want my cock."

"I want you—inside me. Please," I sat up further and ran my hand down his chest and abs and then gripped him between the legs.

"Goddamn it sounds sexy when you say that."

He paused a little before he was about to enter me.

"Please, now, Corbin," I muttered. I couldn't take any more teasing from him. I lay back on the bed, my legs spread, my pleasure totally at his mercy. As I breathed I took in Corbin's gaze, his muscular tattooed body, and his whole essence as he eyed me from above, standing as I lay.

"God damn you are sexy when you beg for it," he growled.

I wrapped my legs around him, tensing slightly and whimpering as he slid his tip inside me. His first thrusts were shallow.

"Ohh baby. You're so tight."

"It's been a while," I blurted out, and instantly wished I hadn't.

"Don't worry, honey. The wait is over."

As cocky as he was, the damn man's words sent waves of pleasure through me.

Corbin pushed all the way in and I let out a loud moan.

He started slow for a few minutes, as I adapted to having him inside of me. After a while, his thrusting quickened.

I dug my fingers into his back, waves of pleasure surging through me.

"You're tense, baby," Corbin whispered in my ear. "So tense. Fuck you feel good…"

One more look into his eyes, and I finally found my rhythm. I let go of it all.

The bad breakup.

A stressful decade.

All of my issues melted away.

I wasn't Eva Napleton anymore.

Tonight, I was simply *Alexa.*

"Yes," I whispered. "God, yes!"

Corbin gripped my hips with his strong hands, forcing himself deeper inside me. I clenched around him, arching my back and moving my hips to meet his thrusts. His body pumped away over mine, our sweaty skin making a *slap slap slap* sound as our bodies met.

After a while he slowed and stopped, gazing into my sex-stare.

"I want you to ride me, baby," he growled.

"Good. Because I want to ride you."

We rolled over and switched positions, without his cock ever leaving me.

I leaned back and moaned as I took him at just the right angle.

"Shit, you're so fucking hot when you whimper like that," he growled as he gripped my arm. I bounced slowly up and down on him, feeling his full length with every movement. I used his body for balance as I fucked him.

"You're about to come, aren't you," he growled as he wrapped his hand around my head and gripped my hair, pulling my face into his for a reckless kiss.

I'd been on the brink for some time now, feeling seconds away. All I needed was a little gentle prodding and I would ripple over the edge. "Yes. I'm close," I muttered.

He slapped me on the ass as he pushed deeper inside me.

"Oh God," I groaned.

"Come for me baby. Come all over me," he grunted.

I screamed as Corbin hit *the spot* again and again.

Clenching around him, I shuddered as I finally let go of everything, reaching my release.

Holy shit was I coming.

This was a full body orgasm. My entire body shuddered as the tingles overtook me.

"Holy fuck, baby," he groaned loudly. I tightened around his thick length as he pulsed and twitched and came inside me.

Our sweaty bodies remained frozen together for a few glorious moments. I collapsed on top of his hard chest, taking deep breaths. My quads burned. Finally Corbin opened his eyes, kissed me on the lips, and helped me ease off of him. I laid down on my back next him, my chest heaving.

A bird tweeted in a tree outside, and I noticed that the sun was starting to come up. *What time was it?*

I propped myself up on my elbows and looked at the microwave. Past five a.m.

Holy shit.

"That was amazing," I said between breaths.

"Yeah, it was," Corbin agreed.

I looked at Corbin's gorgeous naked body in all its glory, standing there in the dawn sunlight. God smiled on this man's genetics. If there was a build-a-man video game, he was what I would build. Ripped muscles. Dimples when he smiled. Eyes that sparkled under long eyelashes.

I went to the bathroom to freshen up. This was amazing, sure, but what happened in Tijuana had to stay in Tijuana. He thought I was Alexa. And that was how tonight would end.

As much as it pained me to say what I was about to say, I had to say it.

When I came out from the bathroom, I looked him right in the eye and told him what was on my mind.

"That was fun. And I think it's time for you to go," I told him as I picked up my undergarments from the floor.

Corbin got up, and for the first time all night, he seemed genuinely surprised, not smirking like an arrogant lady-killer.

"What did you just say?"

"I *said*, Thanks. This was fun. And now it's time for you to go." I picked up my dress off the floor, looked down at Corbin's clothes in a pile on the floor, and back up at him.

"You're kicking *me* out?" he protested, confirming my hypothesis.

"You seem hurt, but let's be honest. What are we *really* going to do here? Are you going to take me out to dinner tomorrow and pretend that you're interested in what I'm saying so you can try to sleep with me again? Or maybe we could date for a few months before it ends? We had our fun. Tonight was fun. Let's end on a high note."

With his jaw hanging open, Corbin tentatively grabbed his briefs, jeans, and shirt. Clearly he wasn't the kind of man who was used to being rushed out. I had a feeling that *he* was the one who usually rushed girls out.

"Um, no, that's not what I was thinking. I just..." Corbin slipped into his jeans.

He looked so damn sexy.

But I knew this was for the best.

He was visibly flustered that I was kicking him out, and not doting over him like most girls probably did. I ushered him toward the door and opened it. He hopped on one foot and tried to put his shoe on quickly.

"Goodbye!" I said. I gave his body a light push, and didn't kiss him goodbye.

"Alright then. Bye Alexa," his low voice reverberated through the hallway outside.

I had to be realistic. What future could we have? What was I going to do, get married to some sexy bad boy I met at a Tijuana club and had a one-night stand with? To whom I didn't even give my real name?

I mean, this was fun, but I worked for the DEA, and something about Corbin screamed shady. Besides, I needed to at least grab a couple of winks of sleep.

3

CORBIN

4 weeks later - San Diego, California

Five. Six. Seven. Eight.

"Ahhh," I grunted as I heaved the weights over my chest. They clinked as I dropped them back onto the rack, and I sat up, feeling the burn run through my arms.

I took a couple of deep breaths and stared outside into the sunlight. For the two years I spent in prison, lifting weights became a kind of mediation for me. Now that I was out and readjusting, I enjoyed my time in my brother's garage weight room even more.

My phone buzzed on the ground and I picked it up.

Three messages, from Lucy, Lacy, and Laura.

One morning selfie in lingerie from the front, one from the back, and one *sans* clothing.

Well good morning ladies.

It had been like this ever since I got out of jail a month

or so ago. Take Lucy's message that went along with her quite attractive selfie:

LUCY: *Hey Corbin I heard you're back in San Diego, when can you come over?*

LACY: *Hi Corbin! Thinking of you now that you're out :)*

OR JUST THE MORE DIRECT:

LAURA: *cum over please*

YEAH, I know. This is not the average guy's text feed. You'd think I was their dick for hire or something. Apparently there is a vast shortage of real men in the southern California area who understand how to give a girl multiple orgasms, so now that I'm back, these girls are ready for the rainy season.

I thought about responding to them, but instead I set my phone back on the ground and pounded out another set of of chest on the bench press.

My mind drifted as I pounded out a few extra reps. The truth was I had a mental block in place these days when it came to women.

And the cause of my trouble, was, of course, a *woman*.

Her name was Alexa, and she ghosted me.

Not even just a standard "oh maybe we'll hang out some-time, maybe not" type of passive aggressive ghost.

After the hottest night of sex in my life, she ghosted *the fuck* out of me. She told me to get out, and she apparently never intended on seeing me again.

I searched high and low for all the Alexa's in San Diego. I even used some of my shady drug connections to look for her.

You'd think in the age of social media, finding someone would be simple.

But this one was good at covering her tracks, apparently.

This was bullshit, and she was eating away at me.

Who has the fuck of their life with someone, and then tells the other person to leave?

Okay okay, I might have done that a few times. But I was at least gentlemanly about it.

Fine, I'm a total hypocrite, I admit it. But fuck this.

I'm the one who does the kicking out. Not the girl. *Me.*

After my workout I showered off and threw some music on my brother's stereo, sat at the kitchen island and had some breakfast. As I was shoveling the last of a delicious omelette into my mouth, I got a text that had nothing to do with a girl. It was my least favorite DEA agent, Ned Ronin.

NED: *What the fuck Corbin. Seriously? You went to Mexico without telling me??*

MY HEART SANK JUST a tad at hearing that. I thought since four weeks had passed, I was in the clear.

CORBIN: *That was four weeks ago. I needed a little escape*

Ned: Get the fuck over here right now, you're in deep shit. We're going to have to do the interview after all

Corbin: See you soon :)

Ned: smh

I SIGHED. Ned was a dick, but I couldn't hate him *too* much since he was the one who got me out of prison early.

Now, instead of Corbin Young, drug dealer extraordinaire, I had to become Corbin Young, undercover agent extraordinaire.

For eighteen years off my sentence, I was willing to do what they asked of me. No fucking way was I going to spend the majority of my life in that shithole known as Folsom Prison.

Today, all I had to do was pass an interview with a lie detecting expert to assure them I wouldn't go back to the dark side.

Piece of fucking cake.

I jumped on my motorcycle and headed over to the headquarters.

Stopping at a red light in the downtown area. I thought I saw a girl who looked like Alexa. Except this girl was blonde, not a dark-haired brunette.

Apparently I was hallucinating. I'd get a grip soon, though.

My mind trailed off again as I thought about that night in Tijuana several weeks ago.

Maybe I shouldn't be so ungrateful about the whole deal. I mean shit, it was my second night out of prison and I went home with the hottest girl in the bar. Her dark hair and lightly tanned skin killed me, just *killed* me. And damn, *those eyes*. I was getting hard again just thinking about her.

Hearing Alexa's moans with her body beneath me reminded me that I was, after two years locked up, a free fucking man.

Emphasis on the *fucking.*

Still. She didn't even let me stick around for a round two. Now *that's* heartbreak—never getting to feel her flesh on my lips again.

The light turned green. *Let it go, man. It's not like you were going to try to hang out with her. You just wanted a hot piece of ass to bang on your second night out of prison.*

I had to chuckle at the fact that I didn't even know Alexa's last name, and here I was still thinking about her four weeks later.

It wasn't about neediness. Hell, I could get another girl in about three seconds flat. So it wasn't about lack of options.

What the hell was it about Alexa that made me still think about her?

Damned if I knew for sure. Maybe I just liked how dirty she was.

4

CORBIN

I poured myself a generous cup of coffee in Ned's office at the DEA's headquarters.

I recoiled just slightly at the heat of the brown liquid, still accustomed to the cold coffee they had served us in prison. "Ned, do you have any cream?"

Ned stared back at me like I had just said the sun was green.

"Cream? You're worried about cream right now? Jesus fucking Christ, Corbin. Jesus H. It's right on the side of the microwave. Jesus." Ned paced around his room with his hands behind his back, too worked up to sit behind his large oak monstrosity of a desk.

"Ah. There it is," I peeked behind the microwave. "You even have those little vanilla flavored cream packets! Hazelnut too! I love these things. Let me tell you Ned, the coffee in prison—I'll be damned if sometimes they just didn't take a little dirt and throw it in the water and heat it up until it was luke-cold. And definitely no cream. Shit no. But sometimes we'd steal a packet or two of butter and make our own...Hey, you look really worked up, buddy. Are you okay?"

Beads of sweat rolled from the corners of Ned's receding brown hairline as he paced back and forth. He had undone the top button of his ironed white shirt and loosened the knot of his tie. His sleeves were rolled up, exposing his hairy forearms as if he had been at the office working through the night on some ball-buster of a problem.

"Corbin, do I look fucking okay to you?" Ned yelled, ceasing his back-and-forth pacing for a moment.

"No, you don't look okay at all. You look stressed. Do you want a cup of coffee? I made extra." I nodded toward the Mr. Coffee and winked at Ned.

"Un-goddamn-believable, Corbin. I get a report from border patrol that says you came over the Mexico/United States border on the second night after your release! After I *explicitly* told you to *stay out of trouble*. And you're yapping on about how much you love little cream packets in your coffee? You just love those cream packets! Is this true or are my sources wrong?"

Ned put his hands on his hips like an angry parent whose kid was in the principal's office.

Except this wasn't a school, and what I did with my personal time sure as hell wasn't any of Ned's business as far as I was concerned, even if it involved bending their "rules."

As long as the DEA needed me to take down Luis Reyes, the most prolific drug dealer of all time, they wouldn't do shit to me, as long as I played ball and got the job done.

And I was a master at getting shit done, be it playing for the dark side or the good side.

I concentrated on putting the third and final cream packet into my coffee while I stood next to the microwave, giving him some time to cool off. I wasn't sure why Ned had such an ax to grind with me when I was basically the heart and soul of this whole goddamn operation.

"Answer me, Corbin. Is this true?" he repeated.

Slowly, I turned around and took a step toward him, holding his gaze.

"It's true," I nodded. "I *do* love cream in my coffee, and these little packets are phenomenal. Ohh, don't get me started about hazelnut flavor. Everyone sees me and thinks tattooed, shady looking guy like that? He's definitely a black coffee guy. But I love cream for my hangover coffee. Isn't it funny how sometimes you don't know what you've got until it's taken away? Now that I'm a free man, I'll even have a latte once in a while or if it's hot I'll have an icy cold—"

"Goddamnit!" Ned pounded his desk with both fists, cutting me off.

"Holy shit. Wow! You think this is funny. Just one big joke about cream in your fucking coffee. Do I look like I'm goddamn laughing? This is the DEA, Corbin! Your early release is contingent on your cooperation. I'm your superior and I'm asking you a question: Did you or did you not roll past border patrol four weeks ago? And some of the reports I gathered from sources in the field are even telling me you went home with some *prostitute?*" Ned paused and looked at his watch, "—for the love of God Corbin, that wasn't even forty-eight hours after your release! If I can't trust you to--"

"Whoa, whoa whoa! That's totally unfair, Ned. Honestly, I'm offended," I said, cutting him off.

Ned took a deep breath and relaxed his shoulders. "Phew. Thank God. So you're saying my sources are wrong. That you didn't break the rules and go across the border to sleep with a prostitute?"

"No, that's pretty much right. Everything except she wasn't just some *prostitute,* Ned! Honestly I thought we had a pretty good connection for one night. And damn, if you woulda seen how gorgeous she was you'd have brought her home yourself. Beautiful dark brown hair, banging body. And this cream-coffee colored skin. It was so soft I actually felt bad that she had to deal with my beard. And I don't usually feel bad, Ned. About almost anything." I took a pull of my coffee and made an audible slurping noise. "Oohh. That's the perfect temperature. Finally. And the perfect amount of hazelnut cream."

I nodded a little, truly content.

"It's the little things in life," I winked. "Am I right? You've got to appreciate them."

Ned looked at me blankly, jaw open, disbelieving of my dripping sarcasm. His eyes widened like they were about to blow right out of his head. Clearly he was used to his agents obeying his every order without question. He brought his hand to his forehead and massaged it with his thumb and forefinger.

"We're out here trying to catch Luis Reyes," he began, his voice sounding dejected, "*the biggest drug dealer of modern times*—and my fucking double agent is more concerned about getting his rocks off than taking this seriously. I swear to God."

"Hey Ned, buck up, pal," I walked over to him and put my hand on his shoulder. He looked like he needed some serious comforting, and not just about the mission. "I'm just trying to fit in, okay? If I'm going to go undercover, I figure I better stick with my old habits in the outside world so I don't arouse any suspicion. Me having a one-night stand with a girl isn't suspicious. You know what *is* suspicious? If I get out of prison and I stop partying like I used to. I just need you to trust me, okay? I'm staying in character. It's all an act." I grinned.

He had to know I was right.

Ned leaned back on his solid oak desk and folded his arms.

"That's exactly the problem Corbin. I don't know if I can trust you. Is this really an act? Or are you just unreliable and unpredictable? I was already skeptical. And after the shit you pulled going across the border, I have my doubts."

I rubbed my short beard with a hand. Two years in prison and a lifetime of crime hadn't exactly turned me into an ego-assuager who would grovel before his superiors. Especially given the dire straits the DEA was in to make a deal with a guy like me in the first place. They'd been trying to catch Reyes for nearly a decade.

"So what are you going to do? Put me in jail and find *another* ex-con who has years of experience working with the Reyes gang? Who spent a year in the same cellblock with one of the Reyes cousins? Get real. I'm all you've got."

"Maybe. But I'm going to take the necessary precautions," Ned cleared his throat, "Which is why I'm bringing one of the DEA's top psychological evaluation specialists to interview you. If you're lying—we'll find out. And we *will* put you back in prison if you're not on our side. She'll be here shortly to deal with you. Dr. Napleton is no bullshit, Corbin. So head out, get some lunch, whatever, and make sure you're back here later."

I took a large gulp of my coffee and swallowed. "She. A girl, huh?"

"Yes Corbin, a girl."

I sat back down and smiled as I held on to my coffee mug. "Alright, I'll do your little interrogation thingy."

Who knew? Maybe she'd be cute.

5

EVA

M y heels clicked on the white tile as I made my way to my boss's office.

For the past month or so, I'd felt like a changed person, and I couldn't put my finger exactly on what made me feel so empowered.

Okay, maybe I could.

Maybe it was the satisfaction I felt the night I kicked the most gorgeous man I'd ever met out of my room.

And all this after I'd spent the night pretending I was another version of me:

Alexa.

After that experience, something just clicked for me about how I'd been letting people push me around at the office.

Instead of retreating into my shell when confrontation became uncomfortable, like I'd done in the past, instead I channelled my inner alter-ego.

I asked myself, *What would Alexa do?*

Sure, in some ways it was a silly mental trick I played on myself.

But it worked. I liked being Alexa.

Alexa was powerful.

Alexa was dominant. She took what she wanted.

She was sexual--but on her own terms. She didn't tolerate the come-ons of imbeciles.

Alexa even had blonde hair--I'd dyed it blonde the Monday after I got back from Tijuana.

"Hello Eva," one of the young agents said as he passed me in the hallway.

"Gabriel," I said with a curt nod and a businesslike smirk.

I had to smile a little at silly thoughts going on inside my own head, and it was definitely giving me the competitive advantage at work.

Today, I had even donned my blue and white pinstripe power suit, my go-to wardrobe choice when I wanted to feel like a boss. It made me look intimidating at best and downright bitchy at worst.

I paused for a moment to look at the plaque on the door before I walked inside.

Ned Ronin: *DEA Head of Operations.*

Like he was some kind of big deal. He'd been in charge of catching Luis Reyes for years, and hadn't even come as close as getting a video of him.

I opened the door without knocking. Ned sat behind his giant desk, clacking away on his laptop, totally engrossed. I didn't think he heard or saw me, which was impressive considering how loud my heels were. I walked up and slammed my palms on his desk.

"Ned," I began. "You're transferring me to the field. I'm done being your psychological evaluation specialist. I've put in my time. And I want the promotion."

He stopped typing and looked at me with an indifferent

gaze.

"We've had this conversation before. We still need you in your current role. In the office. Analysis is your strong suit."

Ned turned back to his computer and started typing again.

"No. Listen to me," I put my hands on my hips and continued. "I've been requesting to work in the field since I first started working here under you—over two years ago. Six years counting all the Ph.D. work I did for the department. You're underutilizing me and you know it! I'm a psychological profiling expert, I speak fluent Spanish, and I've gotten the highest possible score in all of the field tests. Which box don't I check to get into the field and work some actual drug busts?"

"Eva, I appreciate the enthusiasm," Ned continued. "But this is really not the time to talk about this. I'm very stressed. I have bigger fish to fry right now. We have a big project we are ramping up for, or haven't you checked your email this morning?"

My blood boiled at Ned's classic topic bait-and-switch which somehow tried to make me look bad.

Any other day, I might have just backed down and called it quits. He *did* look stressed. And it was early on a Monday. But I had asked about things before, and it was *never* the right time. It was always too early or too late to have this conversation.

I stood tall and channeled my inner Alexa.

Maybe the old Eva would put up with this shit.

But Alexa wouldn't.

Since Ned continued to ignore me, I simply closed his laptop. He slid his hands out of the laptop just before his fingers got crushed. "Hey!" he protested.

"You're not hearing me. You know I'm qualified. I'm

*over*qualified. The last guy you put in the field couldn't even report back to us because he couldn't pass high school Spanish II. He didn't even know *cómo te llamas*. Guess who speaks fluent Spanish, Ned? Me. Yet I'm stuck in the office being your one-trick analyst pony."

"Oh come on. Don't be ridiculous," Ned huffed, opening his laptop back up and pressing the power button. "This isn't your concern."

"Actually, it *is* my concern. It's bullshit I'm not getting the position I deserve just because I don't check that one special box everyone around here needs to get a promotion."

"Oh? And what box would that be? Please, enlighten me, your royal highness," Ned said, leaning back, his voice dripping with sarcasm. He reached to one side of his desk for a cup and took a big gulp of water.

"The special box I don't check," I began, "Is that I don't have a cock and balls," I belted firmly, looking Ned square in the eye. Ned half coughed, half choked on the liquid in his throat. "You okay there?" I reached across the desk and patted him on the back.

"Wrong pipe," Ned croaked. After a few moments he recovered. "Eva, please sit, Sweetie Pie. And seriously, don't be so ornery. Try to smile a little."

My stomach curled a little bit at hearing Ned say that stupid word. I wasn't his *Sweetie Pie*. I wasn't his anything anymore. And yeah, I felt guilty about how and why we ended. But it was over and he had to realize that.

"Ned, don't tell me to fucking smile. This is exactly what I'm talking about. It's inappropriate for you to speak like that now that we've—"

"—stopped dating," Ned interrupted. "I know. Sorry for saying that. It's just a reflex," Ned said. "I got used to it after two years. I didn't mean to make things awkward."

I sighed. Ned might be a bumbling boss, as well as a horrible boyfriend, but he was a nice guy.

A nice guy blocking me from getting what I wanted.

"Well you better get unused to it," I quipped.

"Right," Ned folded his arms. "Let's not get into our past right now. You obviously haven't read your emails today because you'd know that we're about to pull the trigger on Operation Reyes Down—operation D for short. In fact, the wheels are already in motion."

My jaw fell open. "You mean you actually found someone to risk his life undercover who the Reyes family trusts? And who *we* trust?" I shook my head, thinking about the last man they had sent undercover across the border to infiltrate the Reyes headquarters. It didn't end well for him. He didn't make it back and no one ever heard from him again.

"I'm skeptical, Ned. The Reyes family is going to vet the hell out of this guy, whoever we send. Are you sure he has the balls? The connections? And the competence? That's a tall order."

Ned rubbed his forehead with the back of his hand. "We have a guy. We've actually *had* a guy on the books for a full month. This project has been kept top secret though, which is why you didn't know about it. And his résumé is perfect— well, as perfect as we're going to get for this job. A little rough around the edges, but—if we can trust him to stay on our side—he's our guy."

"Who on earth would the Reyes cousins trust? Word on the street is they don't even trust each other."

"The man who we have chosen has earned Reyes's cousin's trust first hand—in prison and outside of prison. We cut eighteen years off of our guy's sentence with a presidential pardon. So he owes us. Big time.

And if he doesn't help us, he's going right back to prison."

"A presidential pardon?" I quirked an eyebrow. "What was he in for?"

"Eighteen counts of cocaine possession, a few of manslaughter," Ned said, handing me a manila folder. "Although his lawyer claimed it was self defense."

"Was it?" I gripped the file in my hand. It was quite heavy.

"Your guess is as good as mine," Ned said, shaking his head. "Like I said Eva, he's a loose cannon, but he's the kind of guy we need if we are actually going to go across the border, find Luis Reyes' base of operations, and extradite the little shit back to the U.S. But we need to be two-hundred fucking percent sure our guy is going to play ball for the DEA and not revert to the dark side. Hence why I brought you in. And if you would have checked your *email* today, you'd know."

"I don't understand. Why didn't you let me know about this operation earlier? You want me to go into an interview cold? I usually prepare for weeks for these things."

"I know, but we've got to get the ball rolling *now*. We received some intel today that lead us to believe Luis Reyes might be going into extended hiding very soon, and if we don't find him soon we could be looking at another decade of searching in vain."

Beads of sweat rolled down Ned's forehead. He was understandably stressed. He'd been trying to take down Reyes for almost two years. If this undercover operation didn't work, Ned was looking at a demotion.

"Eva, I need your expertise here. I need you to interview our undercover guy and find out if he can be trusted. What his motivations are. No one is better at this than you. Do this, and we'll maybe see about getting you into the field at some point in the future I think."

I crossed my arms and shifted my weight back onto my heels. I didn't like all those maybes and probablys. "If I do this, you *will* find a spot for me in the field." My intonation didn't waver. I had given Ned a statement, not asked a question.

"I'll start looking for a spot for you, yes. Something simple to start out. Now I suggest you take the next few hours to review Corbin Young's file. He'll be back here at two p.m. for the interview."

A brick materialized instantaneously in my gut. I cleared my throat. "Did you just say...Corbin Young?"

Ned nodded. "Yep. Heard of him before? The goddamn son of a bitch went to Mexico on his second night out of jail. Can you believe that? My sources told me he left with some broad, possibly a prostitute. What a fucking regular James Dean."

The blood ran out of my face. I opened the manila file and saw Corbin Young's unmistakable mugshot.

"Everything okay?" Ned asked, noticing my silence.

"Okay?" I looked up like a deer in headlights.

He got up from his chair. "With the file, I mean? I just printed that out."

"Oh yes," I said with a forced smile. "Looks great. See you at two."

I stood up quickly and headed for the door. I felt like I might throw up.

"Oh and Eva," he said before I was outside.

"Yes?"

"If you want to move up, knock this one out of the park. Headquarters is going to be observing your skills through the double mirror."

6

CORBIN

The noise of my motorcycle drew dirty looks from a few passersby, but I didn't care in the slightest.

It's hard to give a shit what people think when you're a free man.

I rolled up to one of the first parking spaces and killed my engine in front of the drab red brick office building that housed the DEA.

I got off the motorcycle and removed my sunglasses. The grass surrounding the building was bright green. I'd be damned if San Diego wasn't the best city on the face of the Earth. Seventy degrees and sunny, and I could still taste the delicious turkey, bacon, and avocado sandwich I'd had for lunch when I'd met up with my brother Casey.

Freedom.

A young happy couple walked by on the sidewalk holding hands. I felt so damn good, I gave them a wave. They waved back. I had been on cloud nine all morning replaying that night weeks ago in my mind. I could see Alexa's beautiful brown eyes staring back at me, hear her moans, feel her beneath me. It made no sense. I wasn't the kind of guy who got caught up on a particular girl. It just wasn't my thing. Yet here I was, daydreaming like a middle-schooler.

I entered through the main door of the DEA building and passed through the security check, waving at the secretary who I'd already befriended that morning on my way out. I walked down the hall to Ned's office, and before I could even knock on the door, Ned opened it. I grinned as I walked in.

"Corbin, it's two-fifteen. You're la—"

"It's a touch hot out today, Ned." I breezed past him while he remained standing next to the doorframe. "Do you mind if I grab some water?"

"Sure," Ned answered futilely, pursing his lips as if restraining himself from adding another comment. I opened the mini fridge, took a bottle out and unscrewed the top.

"You guys really keep the beverages stocked around here, don't you?" I took a seat on the small couch in Ned's office and spread out my arms behind me. "So. Analyze me! I'm ready! Do your thing! Where's your psychology girl?"

Ned shook his head and walked back behind his desk. "Please take this seriously, Corbin." He pressed his thumb into his intercom. "Dr. Napleton, Mr. Young is here."

"Coming," said the voice on the other end.

"Corbin," Ned continued, straightening his tie. "Dr. Napleton is the best at what she does, and I want you to treat her with the utmost respect. None of this bullshit cocky attitude that you've had today, getting on tangents about cream in your coffee. Remember, we're getting you out of prison, doing you a big favor."

"You may be doing me a favor," I said. "But the only reason I'm helping you with Reyes is because I think he's a sick fuck."

It's true. I might have been an asshole and a criminal, but even I had standards of honor. Marco Reyes was a sick motherfucker, and the word on the street was that his cousin Luis was even worse. He didn't just go after his enemies, he went after their *children*.

And yeah, there was the matter of the conditional presidential pardon extended to me. Slicing eighteen years off a twenty year sentence was a new lease on life.

The door swung open and a blond woman came in with a blue and white pinstriped pantsuit and an authoritative walk. It was hard to tell because her clothes were so damn businesslike, but my assessment was that she had some nice curves underneath her professional veneer.

She got closer, and I decided I was right. Hell, she almost looked as good as Alexa. Although she had apparently died her hair blonde instead of dark brown, she had the same light coffee colored skin, and these gorgeous brown eyes. She was hot yet proper and—

Holy shit. Were my eyes deceiving me, or was this my goddamn one-night stand in the flesh?

With recently dyed blonde hair. Which was a shame since I loved the way she looked as a brunette. Still, I wasn't complaining about the new do.

Fuck it, I decided. I might as well just come right out and find out.

"Well, fancy seeing you here, Alexa!" I blurted out.

She raised an eyebrow. "Excuse me?"

"Do you two know each other?" Ned interjected, furrowing his brow.

Alexa shot me a look that said *don't you fucking dare*. Like the good poker player I was, I stared back into her big brown eyes and smiled.

I considered my options. I took a guess that a DEA agent

sleeping with a convict was probably against their hand-book or protocol. She could probably get in a lot of trouble for doing what she did with me if I pressed the issue.

Lucky for her, I decided it would be best for me to simply do what I did best: fuck with her. Plus, if the DEA tried to send me back to prison, now I had an ace up my sleeve. A DEA agent sleeping with the criminal she inter-viewed? That certainly made the results suspect.

"Yeah, I've definitely seen you before." I squinted, like I was at the eye doctor trying to read the smallest letters of the eye chart.

"I'm sorry, you must have me confused with someone else." The words rolled off her tongue so convincingly; I began to wonder if maybe Alexa had an identical twin. Except that there was no mistaking how present her scent was in the room.

"Hmmm. It's just that you look...*strikingly* similar to someone I know." I inhaled through my nose deeply, breathing her in.

She took a seat across from me and dropped her note-book onto the table with a thud.

"That's weird. Must be a coincidence. Anyway Mr. Young, my name is Eva Napleton. It's a pleasure to meet you." She extended a slender arm toward me as if she was shaking my hand for the first time, and I couldn't help but smile as I returned her handshake.

She'd somehow transformed herself from the hottest piece of ass at the club to a businesswoman with an aura around her that said *do not fuck with me or I will fuck you up.*

I had to admit, I kind of liked it.

She'd make a new challenge now, as a conquest.

I glanced at Ned, who had seemingly taken my 'looks similar to someone I know' explanation to heart, had moved on, and was jotting something down on a notepad with a blank expression. He had the same nervous, stressed expression that he'd had all day.

"What a weird coincidence. Must be a doppelganger. What a pleasure to *meet you*. You said your name is *Eva?*"

"My first name doesn't really matter, does it? I'm Agent Napleton. Dr. Napleton to you."

So the hot piece of ass was a doctor. That explained a lot. I'd always thought the best lays were intellectual types.

"Oh, I'm sorry," I responded, my tone dripping with sarcasm. "It's just that I've been in prison for so long, I've forgotten when to be formal and when to keep it casual. Will this be our only meeting, *Dr. Napleton*?" I locked eyes with her as I let the syllables roll slowly off my tongue. She brushed her hair behind her ears and diverted her eyes from my gaze. I recognized that tender look in her eyes from earlier. "Or will this become a regular thing? Like weekly, or maybe even daily?"

As her eyes fell on me, my memory flashed to that night when she screamed with my cock so deep inside her I could feel her every movement. In my mind's eye I heard her voice screaming at the top of her lungs as she did that night—the voice that was now speaking so coolly and professionally, it sounded to me like she was faking it, playing a role.

Which half was the real her?

She was a total mindfuck.

And I kind of liked it.

Alexa, Eva—whatever the fuck her name was—sat back in her chair, crossed her legs, and spoke in a professional tone. "It is likely that we will only require one meeting, Corbin. I am the investigative psychologist whom headquarters has assigned to approve you for the operation to take Luis Reyes down. I'll be conducting your psychological evaluation here to make sure you are a suitable candidate for the undercover work you'll be doing with the agency. You look ready. Let's get started, shall we?"

Eva was a doctor who fucked, apparently, like a stripper. It was always easier to put people in boxes, but clearly Eva wasn't someone who was easily nailed down.

Nailed down. Heh.

I pictured nailing Eva again. This time from behind, pressing her body down as I pulled her hair and she screamed my name...

Fuck, I really need to do something about this dirty mind of mine. Thank God this wasn't a mind reader test.

I managed to focus my eyes on Eva's beautiful face. "I think you'll find that I'm a very direct and honest person. I know what I want, and I go get it. Let's start this thing so I can tell you what you want to hear," I took a drink of water and adjusted myself. Surprisingly to many people, honesty was one of my best qualities. I might have been a criminal, but I wasn't a bullshitter.

"Corbin, I'm going to start the digital recorder now," Eva nodded toward Ned and pressed a button on the phone on the table. "The purpose of this interview, as you probably know, is to get everything out in the open. All of the secrets, Corbin. The agency realizes you've had a checkered past and we need to get everything on record."

"That's true," I smirked. "I tend to get into trouble, especially late at night. A few weeks ago, for example, I got into something. I met this girl—a great lay, by the way—but she was a total liar. She didn't even give me her real—"

"Let's stay on topic," Eva interrupted, raising a hand. "There are people who think you're the right man for the job. But we need to know everything about you. Which is why we'll be hooking you up to a lie detector."

"Go ahead." I made a fist and flexed my arm to see how the thing felt. She also hooked up a part that strapped across my chest, and put a little thingy on my finger. I didn't like any kind of contraption connected to my body. It reminded me of the first time I got a lie detector test hooked up to me when I was sixteen, in juvenile jail. I squirmed a little as she hooked it onto me.

"Is your name Corbin Young?" Eva began.

"Yes." I raised my eyebrow, giving her the *are you serious* look.

"How long were you in prison?"

"Twenty-four months, three days, 7 hours."

"You kept track, huh?"

"Not much else to do in prison but count the hours."

"Looks like the detector is working," Eva said, her eyes on the monitor. She scribbled something down on a notepad in front of her. "Moving on to the standard background questions. Growing up, did you torture small animals?"

"I think I forgot to feed my goldfish one night."

I could see her resisting the impulse to roll her eyes. "Do you have problems with authority?"

I smiled. "Depends what you define as a 'problem.'" I made air quotes.

"Let me be specific. Do you have a 'problem' with following orders from Headquarters to take down Luis Reyes?" She imitated my air quotes.

"No. I hate that fucker as much as you do."

"Will you follow all orders we give you, to the letter, without thinking about them?"

"No," I said. "Follow orders blindly? What is this? Nazi Germany? Of course I won't do that."

She nodded and glanced down at the monitor then at

Ned. "Do you more often act on impulse, or do you think things through?"

"Neither. I act on instinct."

"Sounds a lot like impulse."

"It's similar, but different," I explained. "Impulse implies that I am making an uninformed decision. Whereas instinct means that I am taking into account all of the possible angles and making a calculated decision without hesitation. I know what I want, and I take it." I flashed a micro smile in Eva's direction. *And you know better than most people that I get what I want.*

"My, aren't you impressive," Eva says, scribbling some more notes. "This isn't a job interview, just so you know."

She tapped her pen on her pad and flashed her eyes at me. "Just a few more questions."

"Please."

"Do you love anyone?"

"My brother. And what the hell does that have to do with this mission?"

"Those close to you could be in danger for a mission like this, if Reyes finds out your true identity. He might go after them." Eva said. "So you're not in love with anyone? Romantically, I mean."

I scoffed. "Ale—Doctor Napleton. I just got out of prison four weeks ago. That's not a lot of time to fall in love." I stared into Eva's eyes as I said the words. "Besides, I'm not a big love guy. I'm more of a one-night stand type of guy. Maybe two if you're lucky. So don't get any ideas."

"Jesus, Corbin, that's enough," Ned barks from his seat.

Eva sat back in her chair and paused for a bit before asking the next question.

"Did you kill Arnaldo del Valle?"

Coming with the big guns. I knew the question was coming.

Arnaldo's death was one of the man-slaughter counts I'd been charged with.

"Yep. Self defense. We done here?"

Ned nodded.

"Yes," Eva said, taking the equipment off me.

I stood up. "Good. Because it's time for me to meet with Marco Reyes and get this sting started."

"You're meeting with Marco Reyes?" Eva asked.

"Well somebody has to set this fucking plan in motion, and that someone is me."

"Corbin, don't you walk out," Ned barked. "You need to go through us when you are planning this stuff."

I looked at Ned. "I'll let you know how it goes." I turned and walked out the door. These motherfuckers had no idea what they were about to get into. And if this mission was going to succeed, I didn't need them poking around in my business.

7

EVA

Corbin left, and I let out a big breath. I turned to Ned with a businesslike smile, doing my best acting job of holding it together.

"What the hell was that?" Ned asked me from behind his desk.

"What the hell was *what*? We finished the interview like you wanted." My head pounded. There was no denying I was currently stressed.

"No, I mean what the hell was going on there between you two? You added a question, 'are you in love with anyone?' That wasn't on the list of mandatory questions."

Damn. He caught my sly little plan to put that in there. I thought I'd at least mess with Corbin a little. Had to.

"It wasn't? I thought I saw it somewhere," I looked through the list of questions, knowing it was in vain. My mind raced. Sleeping with patients was definitely unethical. An investigative psychologist in the DEA who had slept with a known criminal?

Let's just say it was good to keep that under wraps.

"Jesus H, Eva. I mean the entire interview. The way you

interacted with Corbin. It was simply..." Ned gazed off and out the window, as if searching for some elusive word.

This is it. *Ned knows and he's going to fire me.*

What utter bullshit. If I were a man who had slept with a sexy female criminal, Ned and I would be cracking jokes about her, about how good the sex was, how good we were at bedding women—it would be male bonding. But because I was a female, I was going to lose my job.

I had reached my boiling point. "Stop Ned. I have something I need to say. This isn't fair."

He turned back from the window smiling.

"Fair? It was so simply...brilliant!"

I gulped. "Brilliant?" *Was he serious?*

"Yes, yes. I suppose that's the word I'm looking for." Ned stood and began pacing right in front of me. "I forget, sometimes, why I fell for you in the first place. But seeing you in action reminded me why I...I mean why *we*...had such a spark together when we were going out."

"Ned, please stop. I thought we'd put our feelings to rest after the breakup. I've spent a lot of time moving on, and you should too." Was he really getting into this right now? I'd had enough of going down this road. It always led me to a night of feeling guilty for how we ended.

Ned sat down on the couch in front of me, precisely where Corbin had been sitting. "You were incredible, though! I swear, I thought I noticed that you and Corbin had a certain chemistry. You put him right back in his place, didn't take any shit from him. That's exactly what headquarters is looking for in Corbin's partner."

I clear my throat. "Corbin's...*partner?*"

"Yes," Ned said, folding his hands. "A directive has come down from on high—and they want me to choose an undercover field partner for Corbin. I felt bad for you after what happened between us, so naturally I put your name in the hat. And after seeing how you interacted with him, I want to give you the position...Eva, are you okay?"

I was so lightheaded I had to close my eyes. This time, it wasn't the hangover that was affecting me. Ned's words, the way he emphasized them. *I felt bad for you, so...*

"Eva, you've been wanting to go into the field. I get that. I thought about our conversation this morning. And as hard as it is for me to put you in harm's way, I know it's important to you." Ned leaned forward and put his hand on my shoulder. "I've spoken with headquarters—they called me earlier this afternoon—and they'd like to give you the opportunity to go into the field on Operation D."

Ned left his hand on my shoulder just a bit too long. His next words made everything worse.

"It's just, sometimes, when I get close to you, I feel that attraction that we had coming back. Don't you feel it?"

"Enough," I stood. Ned jerked back his hand, startled.

"Sorry," Ned said.

The reality was that I didn't feel it for the last year of our relationship. And that's why I did the thing I swore I'd never do to someone.

"Ned, I'm sorry, I have to go. I'll let you know about the field." I stood up and walked toward the door. Ned stood up and moved to follow me out. Right before reaching the doorframe, I turned around. "Ned, answer me this. Did you recommend me to go into the field because you think I'd be good at it, or because you feel bad for me?"

I looked Ned in the face, and he lowered his eyes to the ground. I didn't need a lie detector to sense his bullshit. I sighed. Ned didn't think I would be a good field operative. He probably didn't even think I did a 'brilliant' job in dealing with Corbin. This was all just a ploy to get me back.

He felt bad for me. Sure, it was my fault that Ned and I had ended our relationship, but he didn't see me the way I wanted to be seen. I was his little office pet, and he didn't think I could handle myself in the field.

His silence held the answer I was looking for.

"That's what I thought," I said. He took hold of my arm before I walked all the way out.

"Dammit, Eva, this is what you wanted, isn't it? You've been asking me for months to get into the field! Now I give you a golden opportunity, and all of a sudden you have cold feet? Well, I have some news for you: whether it was because I felt bad, or because I think you'll do a good job doesn't matter. I put my neck on the line for you with headquarters. And you walking out on this opportunity is not going to make me look good."

"Let go of me," I said, glancing down at my elbow where Ned was still holding onto me.

He released me. "Fine. I'll give you twenty-four hours to decide if you're in or out. Tell me by this time tomorrow, or else we're going to have to start looking for someone else for this golden opportunity. Tick tock, Eva. Tick tock."

I stormed down the hall, adrenaline and anger surging through my veins.

Outside, I opened the door to my car and pulled my phone out of my purse to answer it.

"Hi, Dr. Napleton."

Speaking of assholes.

"Corbin. How did you get my number?" The way he'd pushed my buttons had me furious. Didn't he know the code for 'we had a one-night stand and that's behind us?'

"Oldest trick in the book, *Alexa*. I made friends with the secretary. What a secure operation you guys are running in the San Diego DEA. All it took was a flirty smile and she basically let me go behind her desk and use her computer. No wonder you haven't caught Luis Reyes yet. Bunch of clowns running the Agency."

I rolled my eyes, but my body shuddered a bit at the name he'd called me.

It was like there was a piece of me only he knew about.

An extremely sexual, badass piece of me.

"I'm surprised you called, and didn't text," I fired back. "Calls are so 2006. It's all about your text game now. Not sure if you kept up your game in prison, or...?"

I could see Corbin's cocky expression through the phone. "Your voice is so hot though, Dr. Napleton. Of course I would call. Besides, I'm an old fashioned kind of guy. 2006 was a great year. I honor the classics."

Silence hung in the air for a moment. "So what do you want, Corbin?"

"What are you doing tonight?"

Is he actually trying to hang out?

"Oh man, I'm really booked up tonight."

"Oh yeah? What are you up to? Spin class? Dying your hair a new color?"

I rolled my eyes. "A whole lot of none-of-your-goddamn-business."

"Ouch! Classic comeback. Well, I'm living at my brother's place on the beach for now. Do you like bonfires?"

I could hear the wind passing by Corbin's voice receiver. He was not getting the message.

"What are you even trying to do? I think I made it clear that our night several weeks ago was a one-night stand. We are not getting together again."

"Okay, I hear you loud and clear. No more one-night stand stuff. Hooking up is off the table. Roger that. So, how about just dinner tonight?"

Relentlessly cocky. As much as a part of me would enjoy another night with Corbin, this could not happen again.

"You're not getting me again. This isn't even an option, Corbin."

"Oh come on. Isn't that the order of modern dating these days anyway? First have sex, then eventually have dinner together after we get to know each other, and then after we've hooked up for a few weeks I go ghost and stop replying to your texts and calls. Don't you want that? It's the great American relationship dream."

I exhaled and stifled a chuckle.

If he was an asshole, he was a funny asshole.

I felt a warm tingle come over my body as I remembered our night in Tijuana. How he pressed me up against the wall. Gently cupped my cheek before he made me come multiple times.

Still, I resisted. This could not happen again.

"Seems like you are adapting pretty well to modern dating for having been in prison for so long."

"C'mon. No expectations...I just want to get dinner and learn more about Luis Reyes' psychological profile. No one knows him--they only know his cousin Marco. Honestly, I don't feel comfortable talking in front of Ned. But for some reason, I trust you. So I'm inviting you over. We should be friends."

"Really? Friends. You can do friends with me?"

"Being honest, I'll want to rip your clothes off as soon as I see you. But if being friends is all you'll give me, fine. I can do that. I'll stay on the other side of the room and we'll talk...just strategize about Reyes. We're colleagues now, so I'll fill you in. I'll text you the time and my address."

A fire lit inside me.

"Fine."

I pressed the red button on my cell and hung up angry. But also turned on. Then angry *because* I was turned on. Even over the phone, Corbin got me all riled up. This wasn't fair.

In my mind's eye, his washboard abs pressed into me, his muscled arms wrapped me up, and I could almost feel myself getting turned on, just at the thought of being with him.

I turned the key in my ignition and ignored the warm tingle that spread through my limbs, and centered in my core.

8

CORBIN

I was on the third story balcony of the beachside penthouse I shared with my brother, sipping tequila on the rocks. I loved the smoky mezcal flavor on my throat and I enjoyed the burn. A gentle warm breeze blew off the beach into my hair.

I watched below as Marco Reyes pulled into my driveway in a yellow Maserati convertible; a deep cumbia beat surging through his speakers. For a man who was second-in-charge to direct the flow of pounds of cocaine per day across the US-Mexico border, he was remarkably indiscrete. A blond bombshell in a red dress was in the passenger seat. Or was her face in his lap? It was hard to tell from the third floor. Knowing Marco's proclivities, I suspected the latter.

Marco stepped out of the car and away from me, appearing to zip up his pants. I saw the red dress sit upright. *Definitely in his lap.*

He looked up and saw me on the balcony. "Ey! cabrón Corbin!"

I smirked at my old drug dealer nickname.

"Come on up. Door is open."

I swigged the last of my tequila and headed downstairs. Marco was just inside the door, hands at his sides. Seeing me walk down the spiral staircase, he let a rare smile fall over his face.

"Corbin, my friend, it's so good to see you."

The girl next to him was a trophy piece that you'd expect to see at one of those car shows in a bikini. She stared down at the floor.

"Likewise." We hugged. A small pang of guilt flashed through me as I looked over his shoulder. But as much as we might want to sugarcoat our friendship, Marco was the reason I got caught and put into prison.

So I felt a little bad about doing what I had to do for the DEA, but he fucked me, and now it was his turn to get fucked.

Funny how knocking eighteen years off your prison sentence can give you some extra perspective.

Although this wasn't going to be easy--not by any stretch of the imagination.

Marco rubbed my shoulders. "I brought you a gift."

He flicked his fingers. "Dixie, give Corbin his gift. *Dale.*" He said the Spanish word with native emphasis, and the girl, who I thought was off in her own little world looking at the floor, smiled at me. She lifted a bottle of something in her hand with a red bow tied around it.

She was one foot short of me. "Mr. Young, I present you this gift. It is *La Suicida Mezcal.*"

Suicida Mezcal was a special mezcal tequila that had long been thought to be extinct. Legend had it that Luis Reyes himself was the maker. The stuff was rumored to have magical, almost cleansing qualities.

I looked at the bottle, and then back at Marco. "I didn't even know they still made this stuff."

He said. "Luis sent it to me. Special, for you."

Dixie took the bottle from my hands and went into the kitchen.

"I didn't think Luis even knows who I am."

Marco gave me the closest thing to a smile his dark soul could muster. "When you were in jail, Corbin, our sales took a noticeable hit."

"I'm sorry to hear that."

"Don't be sorry, this is a good thing. It showed that you are valuable to us."

"So now I'm valuable? That wasn't how it seemed when you were letting me take the fall for that drop off that you fucked up that ended me in fucking jail."

Marco's minimal smile faded, tension filled the air for a moment as we narrowed our eyes at each other.

Dixie broke the ice when she came back into the room with two glasses holding ice and tequila.

"Dixie. Finish the gift," Marco said sternly, the smile rubbed away from his face.

She gave one glass to Marco, and one to me. "Mr. Young, please take me to your room." She spoke the words robotically, reminding me of the *Stepford Wives*.

"Isn't she fucking hot? Take her in the room and fuck her so hard she can't walk straight tomorrow. Give her the Corbin Young *treatment*."

I looked at Dixie. Objectively, she was hot, a legitimate bombshell by most standards. Her red dress barely covered her huge fake tits.

Truth be told, I hadn't managed to get Alexa—I mean Eva—off my mind since the afternoon. I had zero desire to get it on with this girl.

"Thanks for the Mezcal," I said, swirling the tequila. "Sorry, I'm not in the mood for...whatever else this gift entails. "

Dixie's mouth opened in shock when I turned my back on her. Clearly this was not a woman who was used to being turned down for sex. "Besides," I added. "The men have business to attend to, don't we?"

Marco grinned. As much as he liked women, business had always been his first mistress. He could respect the fact that I was blowing off Dixie in favor of man talk. "Let's head up to the balcony." He turned to Dixie. "Stay down here, honey. Man talk time."

We arrived on the balcony and inhaled the fresh ocean air. The sun was about an hour from setting and the red orange glow on the horizon was beautiful. We leaned our elbows on the brick ledge. Marco took a sip of his tequila and stared off into the distance.

"Business has been down, Corbin. We need you. I have a lot of product moving to the area soon. Which is good timing because the new college students arrive next month and they're going to need their fix. And in the last couple of years, we've lost market share without you pushing our brand on campus. I need you to do what you do best."

I squinted and looked out on the ocean. *Do what you do best.* I repeated those words over again in my head.

I took another sip of *La Suicida*. Both of us knew exactly what he meant. I was the king of dealing to the students on college campuses. I'd always been able to win them over and become their number one source.

Sometimes, it got to me though. If you follow the money chain, drug violence in Mexico was fueled by college kids and young twenty-somethings paying prices for cocaine.

Not that it mattered anymore. I was on the Fed's side

now. I had to play this right. I shifted my gaze from the horizon to Marco. "What did you have in mind?"

"We've got a big shipment coming in next week. I want to get you back on the college campuses. Set up shop again, like you did in the old days."

"I'm twenty-nine now, I don't exactly fit right in with the college freshmen anymore," I said.

"You're a young twenty-nine. Especially with the new haircut. And I'm not asking you to *blend in* exactly—I'm just asking you to make connections."

I hesitated, slowly playing my hand. Marco was doing exactly what I needed—bringing me back into his trust circle. I couldn't be too eager though, or it would arouse suspicion. "Marco, you know I'm tainted goods now. I'm lucky I made it out of prison. Sure—we're friends, and I'd love to help you. I just don't know if it's too soon for me to get back into the business."

He nodded. "I can certainly understand your hesitation. But once you've moved this shipment, we'll bring in someone new. Someone younger you can train as an apprentice. But right now we need you. The business needs you." He put a hand on my shoulder. "The family needs you."

Would you send your family to jail for twenty years during the prime of their life? I wanted to say.

Instead I paused to think, sipping my tequila. "This is some good shit. You know what—fuck it. I'm in."

"That's my Cabrón Corbin!" He tightened his grip on my shoulder.

"So what's the total product we're moving?"

"Four-hundred pounds. Eighty-five percent pure."

I did some quick math in my head. "Jesus, Marco. That's over fifteen million dollars street value."

"So you'll do it. You'll absolutely do it?" He sounded like the devil, the tone of his voice bordering between a question and a statement. He stuck his hand out for a shake.

This was the big moment. The grand finale. I had to drop this so natural. Everything was riding on Marco's lack of suspicion at my request to meet the drug lord at the top of the food chain.

An indication of desperation could be met with death.

"I'll do it under one condition."

"What's that?"

"Luis Reyes. I want to meet him."

Marco set his drink down, retracting his handshake. "Why would you need to meet him? We supply the product, you move it. It's simple."

"I know I've always been the dealer. But you are asking me, right after I get out of prison, to take a huge risk that could have me right back behind bars."

Marco lifted his chin. "I'll think about it. In the meantime. This is for you."

He held up a black briefcase and set it on the concrete fence where I leaned on my arms.

"Here is your advance for the work," he said as he popped the thing open. The money smell hit me and I eyed the rolls of hundreds.

"Just some 'get back on your feet money,' now that you're out. And a symbol of trust. After we were in Folsom together for a year, I know I can trust you. And you should know the same. Just do me a favor and be discreet with your spending for a little while. We don't need to draw any unnecessary attention."

He stared at my face, gauging my reaction. I smiled. "You're a good man Marco."

"So you'll do it?" he asked hopefully.

"Get me a face to face with Luis," I said, "and I'm in."

Marco frowned. "I don't understand why this is such a big deal to you."

My heart surged a little bit. "I worked for him for six years. I was his best dealer. I ended up in jail for activities related to his business. I think it's only right."

Marco took a deep breath. "I'll get that meeting with Luis. Give me some time." We clinked glasses and finished the last of our drinks.

On the way downstairs, the topic of conversation turned to women. I told him all about Alexa. Marco asked me every possible question about her, like some kind of lady-killer guru. Creepy bastard.

"Dixie, let's go," Marco said. He turned to me. "We're having a poker match tonight at Cooney's Pub by the beach. Let's go. Starts in an hour."

"Right now?" I balked at the idea, thinking of the plans I'd made with Eva.

"Something the matter?" Marco asked, seeing my hesitation.

"Hell no. Of course I'll come. You ready to lose some money?" Dixie led the way out the door, and I paused. "Be right there."

In the bathroom, I fired off a text to Eva. I was sure she'd understand me having to cancel our little date tonight. She probably didn't care. Like she said, we were just a silly one-night stand.

Nothing more would happen between us.

After one hell of a day, I needed something that I had not indulged in since I was in Tijuana: a drink. After a much needed nap, I met up with Amanda at a bar on the marina downtown. We nabbed a table next to the open window looking out at the water on the other side of the street.

"So let me get this straight," Amanda said, after taking a big sip of her margarita. "Fuckboy from Tijuana—aka the hottie who pretended to be your boyfriend—is an undercover agent."

I peeled at the label of my Corona, my eyes unfocused. "He's not an *agent*, he's an ex-convict. But with how closed off the Reyes circle is, we needed an 'in,' so we had to use him."

It was possible that I shouldn't have been telling Amanda classified information. But she was in my circle of trust, and I always liked to keep her informed on my whereabouts. Besides, as a lawyer, she knew the rules of confidentiality.

"Does your boss—does Ned know?" she asked, we were

still grappling with what to call my boss now that we were broken up.

I took a deep breath and stopped my nervous label peeling to return Amanda's gaze across the bar table. "Ned doesn't know anything. For now at least."

"Only Dr. Eva Napleton would get herself into a situation like this." Amanda's lips slowly curved upward in a devilish smile.

"Uh-oh. I see the lawyer wheels turning."

"Caught in the act. But hear me out. Why would you want to keep it under wraps? If you slept with him, that means you have a sort of power over him. Like how James Bond always slept with the enemy and got insider information." She leaned forward, clearly excited about her James Bond reference.

"I see the logic...sort of. But I'm not sure this is the same thing as a James Bond movie. And I doubt that I have any power over him. I mean, he canceled our plans this evening. Well, to be fair, he begged me to hang out, then I gave in, and then he ditched me."

I couldn't help but feel my heart sink just a little knowing I wouldn't get a chance to see him tonight outside of work hours. Sure, *Eva* was too much of a rule-follower to hook up with him again.

But *Alexa* just might seduce him one more time--just for fun.

"What a dick!" Amanda blurted.

"I know. Very big dick."

Amanda sighed. "Well on the plus side you are proving our hotness vs. asshole theory. I mean, not that it's good that hot guys are assholes. But at least we are right about something. And by the way, I have to ask ...how *was* he?"

I chuckled at the theory Amanda and I had come up

with when we were undergrads at San Diego State. We wanted to do our senior thesis on the correlation between guys who were attractive and how big of assholes they were —something important that needed proving in our twenty-one year old minds. Unfortunately our advisors didn't see the worldly importance of our thesis, and we had to branch off into pursuits in our perspective fields of law and forensic psychology that were more mainstream academically. Still, it was a running joke that we had going, and so far the theory had largely stood up to all of the men we met.

Amanda's phone buzzed and she picked it up. "Speaking of hot guys."

She showed me the message, smiling proudly.

Hey Bambi, this is Casey. I know you're studying abroad right now in Asia, so here's your weekly shirtless selfie.

"See?" She beamed. "I do still have it. The bartender definitely was gay. And can I please respond to him?"

I laughed. I'd forbidden Amanda from talking to Casey after we got back from Tijuana, as much as she wanted to see him. So she made up a story about studying abroad in Asia for an unspecified amount of time.

"Fine," I relented. "

"Yes! I'm going to see what he's up to tonight."

She shot him a quick text, then continued. "Alright, alright so we got a little off topic. You never answered my question about Tijuana, by the way," Amanda said, raising an eyebrow. "How *was* it? For real. You haven't been straight with me about that night. I can tell."

"You know I usually don't kiss and tell."

"Oh please. You haven't had anything to tell lately. Or did you keep a secret from me?"

I clenched up, thinking about the last, and only secret I kept from Amanda: that I cheated on Ned. I was so ashamed after the fact, I couldn't bear to tell a soul. The night it happened I was so drunk and out of it, and Ned had been so distant for so many months that I was loving the attraction I got from that man many moons ago. In my heart I knew my indiscretion was more likely a symptom of a bad relationship than it was a cause of us breaking up, but the fact that I had done such a thing still ate away at my conscience regularly. I knew I should probably have told Amanda of all people, but I just couldn't.

In this instance however, I deemed it a good idea to share with her the gloriousness of kissing Corbin Young. In fact, I didn't know how we had avoided talking about this four weeks after the fact.

"Fine. Now you know I'm not one to make comparisons. But," I leaned across the table and whispered, cupping my mouth with both hands. "It was the best. Sex. Ever. For once in my life, I felt almost..."

"Totally alive?" Amanda said with a perk in her voice. I didn't recall ever seeing Amanda quite on the edge of her seat like she was right now. "I'm getting excited for you, vicariously, if you can't tell."

"I was going to say, 'loved.' But when I say it out loud, it sounds funny. It was like...he was inside my soul. You ever feel that? Although I know you can't love someone from a one night stand," I said.

"Maybe you do, for a moment," Amanda said philosophically.

"Can you call what you have love, if it's only for one moment? Isn't that just lust?" I tried to reason.

Amanda's phone buzzed again, killing the air around the seriousness of my question. She eagerly grabbed it.

"Oh my gosh, he's coming here. You wanna get some weed? He sells it."

"Amanda! I'm a—" I lowered my voice. "I work for the DEA. I can't be out buying weed from street dealers."

"Of course you can. Come on, this is California. Weed's practically more legal than alcohol. Plus, if *you* get caught just say you were doing some undercover research. It's the perfect cover story."

I hesitated. Amanda touched my hand with hers.

"Eva. I have a two thousand page discovery document to read this week. Two thousand. I need some weed to read. Now that is a heck of a rhyme, don't you think?"

She smiled like a six year old who wanted her parent to buy her candy at the grocery store.

I relented. "Fine. So is he just going to come by? Or where do we meet him?"

Amanda looked at her phone. "He says that we can grab an eighth from his contact in the back bar here, and he'll be here a little later. Here, follow me." We grabbed our drinks and walked past the crowded bar toward the back. In the past hour or so the local college students had started to fill the place up.

We walked down a hallway until we reached a steel blue door. A large, bearded Hispanic man with his arms crossed stood as still as a statue next to the door, his eyes on us.

"Hi there," Amanda said to him with a smile.

"Can I help you?" the man replied without uncrossing his arms.

"Yeah. I'm looking for Casey's contact. Casey sent me," Amanda said.

"Yeah, okay. Casey sent me, too," the man said without smiling. "That's what everyone says, lady."

She pulled out her phone with the texts from Casey and showed them to the bouncer. He examined them closely, even pulling up the number attached to the name to make sure she hadn't just typed 'Casey' on any old number in her phone. After a minute he seemed satisfied, turned, and knocked twice on the door. "Hey, Jefe. You got visitors."

"Send them in," said a deep voice with a hint of a Spanish accent.

We bopped in with swagger, feeling good from our drinks. The room was dimly lit, and I could just make out the figures of four men sitting around a poker table through a cloud of cigarette and cigar smoke. Something seemed off. My DEA instincts kicked in. Instinctively I looked for all of the possible exits out of the room. There was the main door behind us, but other than that the place was enclosed like a 1930s speakeasy.

A Hispanic looking man rose from the table and addressed us. I swallowed hard, as I recognized a man who I have only seen in 'most wanted' reports: Marco Reyes.

"Finally," Marco addressed us from across the room. "The whores are here. Come in girls. Shit, they didn't say they were sending a blonde over, but I'll take it."

Marco put his cards down on the table, picked up a handgun, and began to walk toward us blowing out a cloud of cigar smoke. He looked as if like he'd been drinking for hours and couldn't walk in a straight line if he had to.

I felt my heart begin to race.

Amanda didn't know the details of Marco's ruthless background, but even she froze up when she saw his gun, her shoulders tensed. Clearly this was not going to be the easy weed pick-up that we were expecting. I cleared my throat to speak. "Whores? I'm sorry. You must have us confused with someone else."

"Don't play coy with me," he boomed. "We don't hire prostitutes to fucking play games with me all night. We hire them to party."

Marco had deep set eyes and a scar on the right side of his forehead that made him look like a gangster out of a

Scorsese mobster flick. I'd seen his ugly face in countless photos taken by various undercover agents, but never in the flesh. Marco didn't surface much in public. He wasn't at the tippy top of the agency's list of people to capture, but he was pretty high up there, a few dozen spots behind his brother. The reason we hadn't gone after him as hard as Luis was that we figured if we were to nab Marco, Luis could easily find a replacement for him. And whoever that replacement was could be much more violent than Marco, who had a reputation as a man of simple vices: booze and women.

"Hired girls? I'm not sure what you're talking about. We're just here to see Casey." I held onto my smile like a poker face in spite of the pit that had formed in my stomach as Marco waved the gun around.

"We just want to buy some weed." Amanda added. "I'm friends with Casey and—"

"Casey," Marco paused, and stared us down with his dark brown eyes. He spoke grammatically perfect English with a slight hint of a Spanish speaking accent. "is not here. And I've never seen you two in my life. So I'm going to need to see some fucking I.D. Or else you *will* be our whores for the night."

I staved off a shudder. "I.D.? Why do you need to see our I.D.? It's not like we need to be twenty-one to buy weed," I gave Marco a confused-girl baby-face.

He brushed my hair behind my ears with the nozzle of the gun and burst out in a hearty laugh. It was a little awkward, but we managed a chuckle as well—albeit a forced one.

"Did you hear that, boys?" Marco said, turning to the dark corner of the room where the poker game is. "We have a comedian on our hands here. She thinks I'm carding her because she's underage." The men hooted and hollered, shouting at us in a combination of English and Spanish.

I was one step from panic mode. I did my best to channel my inner Alexa.

"You see *mi amor*, you've stumbled into the lion's den, and I do not know who you are," Marco narrowed his eyes, stared at me and then at Amanda. "Our dumbfuck doorman Pablo should not have let you in here. For all we know, you could be undercover cops. 'Friends of Casey looking for weed?'" Marco makes air quotes. "That seems like a fucking made up excuse to me. How the fuck should I know who you are? Casey hasn't told me anything. So that is why I need to see some fucking I.D. Please do not make me ask you again."

I did my best not to tremble. The minute I were to hand over my I.D., Dr. Eva Napleton would come up on a Google search with connections to the DEA. At that point, I would be about as good as dead.

I made a mental note to tell the DEA H.R. department to make me disappear on Google. *A little late for you Eva, don't you think?*

Trembling, Amanda reached into her purse and pulled out her I.D.

Marco snatched it. "Amanda Rogers. 21 Salizar St., Claremesa East. Search it."

My heart thumped and I fumbled around in my purse, pretending to look around for a license I knew I couldn't show him. *This is happening. For Real.*

"I'm waiting for you, pretty one," Marco said, unsmiling, cigar in one hand, gun in the other, smelling like aged whisky. I sent signals to my brain to come up with something good. Right. Now. *Come on synapses, fire!*

I had nothing.

"Looks like you need to clean out your damn purse," Marco taunted as I stalled. "Though I'm not surprised. Most whores are quite unorganized."

"There are about forty-five results for Amanda Rogers, Jefe. I have no idea which one is hers," A high sounding male voice says from the corner.

"Fucking idiot. Search the address," Marco says.

Another voice at the table spoke. "Marco, why are you giving these girls a hard time?" I froze, recognizing the deep timber of the voice immediately.

Corbin. Effing. Young.

Corbin stood up from his seat at the poker table. He was wearing Ray Bans, dark jeans, and a white t-shirt with a deep v-neck that his chest tattoos popped out of.

A tingle ran down my spine as he swaggered over to us. He stopped right in front of me with a smug look on his face. I could see the reflection of my blue tank top and white pants in Corbin's Ray Bans.

"You know these girls, cabrón?" Marco asked confusedly. I held back my utter shock, and prayed that Corbin wouldn't out me.

Ned's words lingered in my mind. *Corbin Young is unpredictable as all hell. That's why we want you to go undercover with him: to keep him under control.*

I was learning that controlling Corbin was going to be about as effective as herding a pride of wild lions.

"What are the odds," Corbin said, raising his sunglasses and revealing his deep blue eyes. He leaned in so he was inches from my body. His smell and even his breath reminded me of what we'd done for hours that night in my hotel room.

"Marco, there's no need to I.D. this bitch," Corbin said nonchalantly.

"And why the fuck not?" Marco scowled. Corbin looked me in the eye for a moment before he turned back to Marco.

"I brought this whore home a few weeks ago in Tijuana. Made her mine." Corbin ran the back of his hand along my hair, tracing the same path that Marco had made with his gun. I straightened my back and stood silent, clenching my jaw. Amanda's eyes widened, though her mouth was closed.

"Her name's Alexa. We ain't gotta worry about her. She's not hired help—she's even better. Just a little drug groupie *puta*. And her friend—" Corbin nodded in Amanda's direction. "That's the girl my brother took home that one night."

Marco broke into a smile. "You slept with her, and you didn't even know she was coming in here?"

Corbin put his hand on Marco's back. "Told you I haven't lost it. How the hell am I supposed to keep track of all the girls in San Diego with beautiful booties that my brother and I take home?" Corbin cocked his head and darted his eyes to me with a smirk.

Marco scratched his head with the nozzle of the gun. "No shit. You'd have to list off half the town!" The guys at the poker table got a kick out of that one and broke into laughter again.

"That mocha skin and those slightly darker features— She's a rare specimen. You have Mexican blood in you, I can tell. But there's something else too," Marco said.

"My dad is Irish and my mom is part Mexican. I like to say I'm 'Mirish.'" I performed a weird movement resembling a curtsy. I had no idea why.

Marco tucked the gun back into his waistband. "Well shit. Forget about the I.D. thing, Alexa. Corbin's word is gold. And I gotta ask, Corbin. Can I try her?"

I gulped. *Did he just say 'try me?' Like I'm a damn cocktail?*

Corbin laughed. "Maybe later, Marco. Tonight, she's

mine again. Isn't that right. *Mi amor.*" He said the words in a mocking tone, and then slid his hand down my side until his palm landed on the back pocket of my white pants and cupped my ass. Out of the corner of my eye, I saw Marco's vision dart to where Corbin's hand was touching me.

Marco took a puff of his cigar and blew out the smoke, shaking his head. "Of course, the Young brothers *would* have a monopoly on the prettiest girls of the night." Turning to Corbin, he continued. "You'll have to show me where you get girls like this sometime."

"How he got *me*?" I said, a little taken aback. Why is it always the guy going after the girl? "Oh, please, Corbin didn't have any special—"

In the middle of my sentence, Corbin pulled my body into his and covered my lips with his own. One of his hands gripped my hips and pulled me into him. As infuriated as I was, electricity coursed from Corbin's body through mine when he touched me. I reciprocated the kiss with passionate anger bubbling inside me. I dug my nails in to Corbin's back through his shirt. Why did this asshole get me so fired up?

And so turned on.

Corbin let me go and turned toward Marco. "The problem with this one is she just doesn't know when to keep her fucking mouth shut."

"Isn't that the truth about the pretty ones, cabrón?" Marco said, smiling broadly at me and rubbing his hand on his gun. "Alexa, you are lucky to be the property of such a powerful man. Or else, who knows what would become of you."

A solid percentage of my brain wanted to slap Corbin Young, the arrogant pig. How dare he!? Touching me, kissing me at will. His *property*?

And then, of course there was the other part of me: the part that wanted him to jump right back on top of me.

Why on earth do I want him so badly?

Amanda and I's proposed senior thesis was so spot on. The bigger the asshole, the more I wanted him.

"So what did you girls come in here for any way?" Corbin said. "Jesus, we've gotten off topic. Some weed, was it?"

Amanda nodded. It was weird seeing her so much more timid than her normal confident lawyer self.

"Douglass," Corbin motioned toward the poker table. "Weigh her out an ounce."

"Give her the special groupie price," Marco added.

"What's the special groupie price?" Amanda asked.

One of the men at the table tossed a plastic bag of weed at Corbin. He caught it and handed it to Amanda.

"It means you just have to go enjoy one drink at the bar, before you leave, and the weed is free," Marco said. "Just don't forget to grab that drink. Because if we have time we might even join you, if we finish this game soon."

"Seems like an odd system," I retorted with a little bit of attitude.

I turned to go but I felt a slap on my rear as I was leaving. I flinched and wheeled around. All the guys at the table were laughing. Corbin and Marco stood equidistant from me, so it could have been either one of them. Corbin winked.

"Good to run into you again, *Alexa*. Run along now. Man talk," Corbin growled, an gave me another pat.

I managed to smile on the outside despite how hot my blood boiled on the inside.

❧

"WE SHOULD GET out of this bar, don't you think?" Amanda said as soon as we were back in the main area. The song *Should I Stay or Should I Go* played over the loud noise of the bar as the evening crowd rolled in. "That was too crazy. The way Marco was waving the gun around, it was like a scene out of my worst nightmares. Let's go. I don't think this one more drink thing is a good idea."

I was about to open my mouth to agree with her, but as if on cue, a very tall, sandy-blonde haired man walked into the room. Heads turned as the man walked past the crowd, especially given that he was a full six inches taller than almost everyone in the bar. "Hello ladies," Casey smiled and kissed Amanda on the cheek, her eyes lighting up like diamonds in the sky.

"Casey!" Amanda said, hugging him. We weren't leaving just yet.

A cocktail waitress walked over with a whiskey colored drink in her hand. "Hi. Are you Alexa?"

I nodded. "Yeah. Why?"

"This manhattan is for you. It's a house specialty. Compliments of Marco. Enjoy," she said and handed it to me.

I took a sip. "Oof. It's quite strong." I recoiled a little bit at the taste.

"Marco says it's special for you," the waitress added.

"It's fine," Casey interjected. "He always buys drinks for girls who pick up weed from him personally."

"Oh yeah? Well does he also wave a gun around in front of them?"

"He did what?" Casey furrowed his brow.

"It's okay," Amanda added. "Your brother came to the rescue, so to speak."

"I guess I'll finish this one drink," I said. I didn't feel like giving Casey a full explanation of Corbin and I's day full of strange coincidences. "And then I'm heading home."

I needed to get home, get some rest, and process what just happened. I figured I'd leave these two little lovebirds alone to do their thing.

11

CORBIN

After our poker game was over, I walked back into the bar and looked for Eva, but I didn't see her anywhere. I texted her too, but no response.

So I walked in the cool air along Mission Bay with the lights from the San Diego skyline bright in the night. I had to wonder what Eva thought of the little performance I put on in front of Marco and the guys.

I took a cigarette and lighter out of my pocket. Cupping my hands to block the wind, I lit it and inhaled. I wasn't normally a smoker, but after the day I'd had I needed a few drags to clear my head. I walked up to the shore's edge and sauntered onto one of the open docks. Sitting on the edge of the wood, I let my legs hang out over the water as I considered what a crazy day it had been, even by my standards.

Evidently the day wasn't finished being crazy, because a voluptuous prostitute in high heels and a black dress walked by on the boardwalk and began to hit on me.

"Hey honey! For a cutie pie like you I'll give half price!" she called in an accent that I couldn't quite put my finger on.

"No thanks," I said. The prostitute didn't waiver. She came closer and sat down next to me as I took another puff.

"Well how about a spare cigarette?" she asked. I handed her one of my Marlboros.

"Corbin," a female voice spoke behind me. I whipped my head around, burning cigarette held loosely between my lips.

Eva Napleton stood in her pretty little white pants and the blue tank that clung to the voluptuous top half of her body, her blond hair blowing a little in the wind. A street lamp lit her face up.

As if the last twenty-four hours wasn't already full of enough goddamn coincidences.

"Oh hi there Alexa. I mean Eva. Or should it be Dr. Napleton? I'm so confused these days." I turned toward the prostitute and cocked my head in the universal *get out of here* sign. "Take a hike," I said since I wasn't sure if she would catch my body language.

The prostitute took off down the boardwalk, her heels clomping on the concrete as she walked off.

Eva came closer and joined me on the dock, letting her feet dangle over the water. She didn't say anything, though. Maybe she was trying to process everything that was happening just like I was.

I exhaled the smoke from my cigarette toward the sea, and then turned to look her in the eye. To be honest, all I wanted was to rip her clothes off right there, right then, and do the same thing we had done four weeks ago. By the water under a full moon didn't seem like such a bad place for a round two.

"You are un-fucking-believable, you know that?" I said instead.

Eva glared at me with those sexy damn brown eyes.

"Was all that verbal abuse really necessary? Not to mention the physical stuff."

I squinted at her and took my cigarette out of my mouth for a moment to flick the ashes off.

I just saved this girl's ass from a certain death and she was giving *me* a hard time?

"You know what? You're right. I should have just said, 'Oh, hello Dr. Eva Napleton! Nice to see you! What did you think of that interview in the DEA today? What a surprise to see you here! You want to play some poker with us!?'"

Eva folded her arms. "Don't patronize me. Ass."

I didn't break off eye contact. "I'm not patronizing you. I'm making a point. Marco and the rest of those guys—they don't exactly have twenty-first century sensibilities when it comes to gender roles. That's just how they treat women. I had to make sure I got my point across—that you're mine and they can't touch you. If you can't handle pretending you're my mistress—well shit, that's your problem, not mine."

"But you didn't have to take it so far!" Eva threw up her hands. "The ass slapping in front of them. Grabbing me however you wanted. Sure, when we're hooking up that's all good, but you were treating me like I was a..."

"A whore?" I completed her sentence.

"You know what? Fuck you, asshole."

Frustrated, she got up and walked a few steps away, giving me the view of the back of her sexy body. The high-heeled prostitute, who was standing about thirty feet away now smoking her cigarette, smiled at her and then glanced at me again.

I got up. "Oh, I'm sorry Eva. Did I pass your hard limits? Did I play a dirty trick on you? Because you seemed pretty okay with it when I was deep inside you in the hotel room that night."

"Maybe you're right. I did like it. But that was a one time thing, and you're still an asshole," Eva said, pacing back and forth.

"So the fact that I saved your ass by slapping it a little too hard and making sure Marco doesn't suspect anything makes *me* an asshole? Spare me the logic. I'm done here. What's the point in even talking to you? You're drunk. Besides, you're right. I *am* an asshole. I'm an asshole and a lady killer. Always have been, always will be. Sorry I'm not sorry that I tell it like it is."

The words spewed like venom from my mouth. I didn't mean for them to sound so scathing, but there was definitely some truth in them.

Eva was still pacing, but I could see her swaying. And it was not windy. Something was not quite right with her.

"I can't believe the balls you have, saying that I'm drunk. I had two drinks tonight—two. And—"

"You're so cute when you're angry," I interrupted. My phone buzzed and I took it out to look at it.

"Oh, is that another one of your hookups?" she scoffed. I read the message.

"It's Ned. He says...holy shit!"

My grip tensed as I read the words.

"What it's say?" she asked.

"He says I'm going undercover with a partner to Mexico. With *you*."

Eva nodded, and smiled like a goof. "Ima go undercova with da big daddy."

I cocked my head, a little confused as to why she was suddenly slurring her words so badly.

"No," I continued. "This is unacceptable. Marco does *not*

take kindly to outsiders. No way he'll let you come with me. Besides, we don't even know how we're going to find Luis Reyes anyways. I don't even need you."

Eva stepped forward and put her hand on my chest.

"Y-Y-You don needa me? Awww. T-t-that's too baa-aad." She leaned her chest into mine, and I felt a jolt of adrenaline flow through me as her smell reminded me of our night together. She looked up at me, batted her lashes, and got up on her tippy toes to whisper in my ear. "I don needa you, but I w-w-*want* you Corbin Youngggg. Again and again and...You make me soooo..."

Trailing off, she got off her tippy toes and tried to smile at me, but something was off.

"Eva, are you okay?"

Her eyes rolled to the back of her head, and I grabbed her body in a bear hug to keep her from falling. "You don't, I don't...I d-d-don't," she slurred her words and her knees wobbled.

"Eva! What's happening to you?"

Eva's body went entirely limp, her legs like spaghetti. I scooped her up in my arms.

"Eva? Eva!?"

12

EVA

I opened my eyes to find myself in a bed that I didn't recognize. Outside, I could hear seagulls. The salty air smell wafted in through an open window. I was as thirsty as someone who had just finished a desert walk.

I sprung up in bed and looked around to see myself in a mostly bare room with white walls and very minimal décor.

Where am I and how the hell did I get here?

My head felt like it had just gotten hit by a ton of bricks.

Dammit. It had probably been since college that I'd found myself in one of those figure-out-what-you-did-last-night adventures.

Last...memory...think...hard.

The bar! Right, I was at the bar with Amanda, and we met Marco. Marco gave me that free drink and then...

My heart pounded as I ran through worst case scenarios. *Did Marco take me home? Is this Marco's place?*

I ripped the covers off and saw that I still had on the white pants from last night. My blue tank top rode up my waist. It comforted me to know I probably kept those on.

Thank God for tight white pants that were too hard to rip off.

The doorknob rattled and I instinctively dove behind the bed. I looked for sharp objects, anything that could be used to defend myself. I saw an Italian dress shoe size fourteen beneath the bed, so I grabbed it in my hand and peeked my eyes over the top of the bed.

"I didn't know you were a vampire, scared of the light and all."

Corbin.

Apparently I couldn't get rid of this man, no matter what I did.

I stood up and saw him in the doorframe wearing athletic shorts and no shirt, holding two mugs, his v-shape not going unnoticed. The aroma of fresh coffee wafted through the air. I breathed an audible sigh of relief and dropped the shoe to the ground.

I'd never been so excited to see an asshole.

"Did your feet grow in the night?" he asked, his eyes tracing my hand that dropped the shoe.

"Um, you know what? That's a possibility given that I don't remember much from last night. Did we..."

"Have sex? Funny. I like my women lucid and eager. Not drugged. Besides, those pants are so damn tight. I left you in the bed and slept on the couch. Coffee?"

I felt an overwhelming sense of both relief that we didn't do anything, and embarrassment that I'd forgotten the night.

"I do have a few questions. A lot of holes in the night," I said, and turned to look out the window. "Nice view by the way. We're on the third floor? I'm surprised you got a place this nice right out of prison."

Corbin cocked his head and gave me a funny look. "You don't remember going on the balcony last night?"

"No."

"We had this exact same conversation."

A brick formed in my stomach.

"Looks like I have a lot of holes to fill in from the night." I took a sip of the warm brown liquid in my hand. "My memory is hazy, but I remember someone giving me that drink compliments of Marco, and then...I think I saw you go home with a prostitute?"

"You don't remember anything." Corbin said matter-of-factly, a sip of his own coffee and nodded calmly.

I shook my head.

"Well, Ned sent me this text."

He pulled out his phone and I read his screen.

Hi Corbin. Eva will be joining you undercover. Let's come up with some possible undercover identities for her to go with you. Maybe your cousin who is looking to get in on the business?

I almost spit up my coffee.

"I'm your cousin who is looking to get in on the business?" I repeated aloud. "That's about the dumbest cover story that I've ever heard."

"You're telling me," Corbin agreed.

Corbin made a sipping sound and nodded at me. The cup looked tiny in his massive hand.

"Can I be frank with you for a moment?" I asked.

"I prefer you as Alexa, but you can be whoever you want with me. I do like role playing, and being Frank sounds like an interesting character choice. Let's run with it."

I rolled my eyes. "This is serious, Corbin. I can't go undercover with you because I don't *trust* you. I looked up your file. You didn't even mention the fact that you were a convict when we hooked up the first night. Or that you killed a person. You lied to me."

Corbin laughed out loud. "You're getting mad at *me* for lying by omission? Might I remind you that you told me—ahem—a fake fucking name."

"Touché. But that doesn't matter. I did that for my own safety—so that you wouldn't be searching for me or something on social media. I didn't think we would end up going home together, I thought I'd only mess with you for a few minutes. Besides, a person's name is different—you left out things about your *character*. It's not the same."

"Well it's too bad you feel that way," he said. "Because I was actually starting to enjoy the idea of bringing you undercover with me as my mistress sidepiece."

My blood boiled, and I choked a little on my coffee. "Your *mistress sidepiece?* No no no. That is not happening. Absolutely not."

"You're funny," he said. "Do you *not* remember me saving your ass last night from Marco by treating you as my mistress? That's the only person you'll be in front of Marco and his criminal associates from now on. Try anything else, and it will be incredibly suspect."

I bit my lip and resisted grinding my teeth, because Corbin was right.

"I guess I'm still piecing together last night. Marco put something in my drink, I'm sure of it."

I stared at the tattooed man in front of me, feeling infuriated. No one in my life had managed to make me that angry while still wanting to jump on top of him. It wasn't fair.

Corbin took a step toward me and ran his hand through my hair. "On second thought, it's probably best that you don't come with me. I mean I'd love to go undercover with you. It would be a fun few days, but I just don't think you could handle it. You wouldn't be able to get in the role. You just wouldn't last. It's alright. Not everyone is cut out for this type of work."

"Goddamn it, I can't fucking win, can I," I shook my head, feeling stuck between a rock and a hard place. I could either go undercover *as a man's arm candy,* or I could say no, turn down the role, and who knew when Ned would offer me another chance to go undercover?

I looked toward the window. Corbin walked over to the venetian blinds and yanked them up, allowing light to stream in. "I don't get why you're so offended. This has nothing to do with your education. You're a smart fucking girl—that's obvious. A lot fucking smarter than a non-college educated thug like me. But you got so damn angry last night at me for just making sure those guys knew you belonged to me, so they wouldn't fuck with you. I've been around these types of people my whole life, and they are experts at seeing through bullshit. So *no*, I don't think you would last. And I don't want you to get hurt."

I rubbed my face with my hand. I hated to admit it, I *had* freaked out a little last night, even before Marco had (proba-bly) drugged me. And it wasn't that I had really been offended by anything he said. Maybe I freaked out because I really *liked hearing him say those things.*

"Wait a second," I said, echoing Corbin's last comment in my mind. "Did you just give me a compliment about my intellectual ability?"

"Yeah, it's hot that you're smart. Probably much too smart for a thug like me. Don't go and get all uppity on me though, okay?"

I let a smile escape my lips. In spite of Corbin's lack of

formal schooling, the DEA had rated him one of the most intelligent criminals around today. But I decided it was best not to share that information. I didn't want his ego getting any bigger.

"I need to shower off. Where's your bathroom? Do you have a towel?"

He pointed me in the direction of the master bathroom. I entered and turned on the water to heat it up. Corbin fetched a towel from his closet and brought it to me.

"You're right about last night," I said, wiggling out of my pants. "I freaked. But it wasn't because I can't perform under pressure. I'm just feeling a little weird about the whole me-and-you thing. We never talked about it. To me, you were just supposed to be a one night indulgence. I can't have this affecting my career. Ned or anyone."

"What me-and-you thing?" Corbin winked. "What happens in Mexico, stays in Mexico. Never happened. I've forgotten all about you kicking me out." I noticed Corbin's eyes were following me.

"Oh stop it already," I said. "You act like you were going to try and wife me up, and then I kicked you out to end your fantasy. I was just some club girl who you got your rocks off with on the second night out of prison. Admit it."

"Maybe," Corbin said with a wry smile. "But now I've decided I'm not done with you."

"That doesn't matter. Because I'm done with you. Seriously."

I took off my bra and hung it up. I was getting ready to take my panties off when I noticed Corbin was still staring at me, slowly hanging the towel up on the rack next to the shower.

"What are you looking at?" I said. "It's not like you haven't seen me naked before."

"It was dark that night," Corbin smirked. "You're sexier in the light. Plus, one time is not enough with you, *Alexa.*"

He took a step toward me so his body was inches from me. I could feel the heat radiating from his body.

I wanted him to touch me so badly. Just take me again.

"Don't do this," I said.

"Do what?"

"Dammit, Corbin, you know exactly what. Don't."

He took hold of my hips and pressed his bare chest into the flesh of my breasts, his eyes staring into mine, lips curved upward in a slight smile. I thought of all the reasons why this couldn't happen again. Reasons like my career and my future. Good, solid reasons. I tried to picture anything but the criminal forcing his body onto mine, making me moan. But I could feel him through his shorts, growing harder, and it was making me salivate.

"All I'm doing," he said, stroking my hair, "is checking to see if you're able to convincingly play my mistress undercover."

"And?" His big hands moved from my hips to my ass, and he palmed my cheeks.

"Seems to me like you could do a pretty good job. But you'd have to step into the role a little bit more."

"Corbin, no," I put my hands to his chest and pushed him off. "I can't go undercover with you. Now please leave me so I can shower, and then you're taking me home."

"Fine," Corbin finally backed off, turned around, and began to walk out of the room. Before he closed the door, he turned to me. "I'll be waiting outside in the car to take you home. Have a nice shower. And oh, I left cut up some pineapple for you and left it on the kitchen island. It's a wonderful hangover cure."

With that he was finally gone, and I breathed a sigh of

relief at being able to resist his charms. I took off my panties before stepping into the shower.

They were as wet as if I'd gotten in with them.

13

CORBIN

I sat in the driver's seat of my brother's SUV waiting for Eva to come out of the penthouse so I could drive her home. It was a typical seventy and sunny morning in San Diego, so I put the key in the ignition, rolled down the window, and turned on the radio. A new Kanye song played and I didn't even recognize it. It was funny how a couple of years in jail could make you completely out of the loop when it came to pop culture.

I took a deep breath. I had to get out of there after seeing Eva almost nude again. There was a monster inside me, and I knew how badly it wanted her. I was never intimidated by any woman, but the way Eva had no problem stripping down in front of me—with utter confidence—made me need to get the hell out of there, away from her. I was having a hell of a time keeping my hands off her.

Last night after she passed out on the dock, I carried her to my room and tucked her under the covers. She looked so damn sweet sleeping there that I wanted nothing more than to cuddle up to her. Instead, I slept on the couch.

A cold, hard, realization hit me. Just some passing words

that my jail psychologist had said to me, but now rung truer than I originally thought. *Corbin, when you really love someone, you run. It's because your mom left you when you were young, and you never knew your dad.*

I've never been someone who believed in the Freudian analysis bullshit, but maybe he had something there.

I tried to think about what Eva was making me feel—but processing my own emotions had never really been my strong suit. I was the king of wham-bam-thank-you-ma'am's. I'd never cut up pineapple for a girl before.

Was I seriously making a big deal about cutting up pineapple for a Eva as some huge, selfless gesture?

What a silly act to make into a symbol.

It was true, though. I'd been selfish as hell throughout my life. Aside from my siblings—who I would die for no question if it came to that—I believed that people were really, truly, better off without me, *especially* women. I'd tear through them like the Tasmanian devil, giving them a few nights they'd never forget.

And then I'd stop calling. They wouldn't.

The door to the penthouse swung open and Eva appeared, jolting me from my thoughts. She wore some old blue sweat pants of mine and a white t-shirt, no bra. I couldn't help but stare at her curvy body as she walked toward me in the sun like some kind of cheesy B romance movie scene. She was knockout gorgeous without even trying, which was infuriating. I reached over and popped the passenger's side door open for her.

"I hope you don't mind, I didn't much feel like squeezing into those pants again, so I raided your dresser and found these," she said as she hopped into the front seat.

"Keep 'em," I said as I kicked the car into drive.

"You're doing pretty well for yourself for having just got out of prison. A motorcycle *and* an SUV?"

"It's my brother's," I said, pulling out of the driveway.

"Oh really. Well it's nice. What does your brother do?" Eva cocked her head toward me.

"Don't worry about it. It's not important," I said. I didn't feel like getting into my brother's profession, which always yielded ten million questions as soon as girls found it out.

"I think it is important. Very relevant, in fact. How am I supposed to trust you if you won't even tell me a simple detail about your life? Here, I'll start. I have one brother who lives in Chicago. His name is Jake. We grew up poor on the south side. I got out of there to start new and ended up at San Diego State. I was raised by a single mom, and I haven't seen my biological dad in years. See? That wasn't so hard. Now you."

I drove in silence for a moment. We pulled up to a red light and I glanced over at her. "I appreciate your family tree honesty, but you don't want to know about me. No one does. Trust me. It's not a fun story. Just depressing. Wait...holy shit. Do you mean *The* Jake Napleton is your brother? Like the baseball MVP of the league last year?"

She nodded.

"Holy shit," I added.

She put her hand on my knee. "So are you saying my story wasn't depressing? My brother and I are self-made. We're two of the only people from our neighborhood who made it out."

I shrugged.

"Anyways, yes, I do want to know about you," she continued. "You've piqued my curiosity. This isn't an act. I'm genuinely curious. What drives a guy like you to get into dealing drugs at a young age? And can I trust you on the other side of the drug war?"

For years, I'd been trying to get over my past. I just wanted to forget about it. My upbringing was far from stellar. But she was looking at me with a look that conveyed true interest.

She had no idea what she was about to get into. My life had been a shit show up until...

I was going to say 'Now,' but it really was still a shit show. Who knew if I'd ever be out of the woods.

"If you insist," I growled as I jammed my foot on the accelerator and hung a right at the corner to take a detour. Eva fastened her seatbelt. "It's time for the Corbin Young roots tour."

"Where are you taking me?" she asked, suddenly sounding a little scared.

"You're completely right," I said, ignoring her immediate question. "You have no reason to trust me at this point." My eyes were glued to the road as I sped on. I gave a token pause at a stop sign before blowing through it. I turned left on a dirty old road with lots of potholes, the same ones since the nineties when I grew up there. "I want to teach you a little bit about my life so you understand where I'm coming from. Do you know where we are right now?"

"Of course I do. We're in Vista Chulo. I have an uncle and a..." Eva paused, like she was remembering an old friend. "...a cousin who used to be from here," she trailed off.

"Where does your cousin live now?" I asked.

"Javi's not with us anymore," she said, glancing at the cross dangling from the rear view mirror.

"I'm sorry to hear that."

A tear streamed down Eva's cheek, and she immediately

wiped it away, pretending that I hadn't seen it. I massaged her shoulder for a second, and slid my hand down her arm and did something I hadn't done in years: I held her hand just because I wanted to.

Fingers interlocked, we drove on in silence for a few moments.

I pulled over in front of a dilapidated red brick duplex wedged between two larger houses and put the car into park for a minute. I rolled down her window with my controls and pointed outside. "This is where me and my brother and sister grew up with my mom. It's a tiny house, obviously. We had one bedroom between the four of us. I slept in a bunk bed with my brother, my mom slept on a futon couch in the main room, and my sister had her own room."

Eva looked shocked. "Does your mom still live there?"

"Not since she left when I was fourteen."

Eva's eyes widened. "She just *left?*"

"She battled with drugs her whole life. Finally, the drugs won. I think she figured we were better off without her." I swallowed, and took a deep breath. "Like I said, not a pretty story."

"What did you *do?* Like for money?"

I shrugged. "I started selling coke. I had a little brother and sister to raise. And I wasn't about to go to child services, let them split up the family or whatever they would do to us."

I felt her squeeze my hand. She turned toward me and looked me in the eye, running her free hand from my forearm up my bicep to my shoulder.

"Corbin, you know none of this was your fault, right?"

"Yeah, of course not," I said, not really considering the words. Eva was getting all mushy on me and I was done opening up.

I kicked the car out of park and pulled off down the road. It wasn't even noon yet and we both could easily spot the crack dealers who were circulating down the sidewalk, getting on with their unique brand of sales.

"See that corner over there?" I pointed to the intersection ahead of us. A few teenagers stood there smoking cigarettes and loitering by a corner gas station. Eva nodded. "That's where we saw our first drive-by shooting when I was eleven and Casey was nine. We heard some pops, came outside, and saw a guy bleeding out on the concrete."

"Jesus, Corbin, that's awful."

"It's also the same corner I sold my first dime-bag when I was thirteen. Ironic."

Eva seemed to have a visible, visceral reaction to my comments. Her body squirmed in the passenger's seat.

"Why are you showing me these things?" Eva asked, still visibly shaken. "How is this going to make me trust you?"

I looked over at her and I had to smile. "I'm not sure how. I've never really told anyone about these things. The truth is I'm ashamed of the way I've grown up. I've always tried to hide my roots. I've done my time on the wrong side of things. But moving forward, I'm ready to do whatever it takes to put an end to this awful ring of crime and take down Luis Reyes. I know we had one crazy night together— before we knew who each other were. But a lot has happened since then. And I'm willing to put aside my past, as well as whatever it is that we have between us, if it means taking down Reyes."

I could feel Eva's eyes searing into me. She was probably wondering if she could really trust me, if I had changed my ways. It felt oddly liberating to be this honest with her. I decided that I liked being open with Eva. Maybe I would keep doing it.

My grip on the steering wheel tightened as I stopped at a red light. A convertible pulled up beside us.

"Hey cabrón!" yelled an unmistakable voice. On our right, Marco Reyes rode in a red convertible with a dark haired girl who sat silently in the passenger's seat. "Nice to see you in the neighborhood today! Your mistress ran out on me last night so I decided to get another one."

I ignored his reference to Eva, who was sitting silently between us. "Blonde yesterday, brunette today?" I asked him, nodding toward the girl next to him.

"New girl for every day of the week. You know all about that, don't you?"

"Variety is the spice of life."

"Exactly. Although I haven't had a girl like her lately." Marco smiled at Eva. "Alexa, you said your name was? I was so sad when I came out to look for you and you were gone last night."

Eva held onto her plastic smile. I shot her a look. *Just play. The fuck. Along.*

"I would never do anything to disobey my *papi*," she said, pursing her lips and running her hand over my chest. *Wow. Nice Spanish accent. Plus one point.*

"Now that's the kind of girl I like: an obedient one. You're a lucky man, Corbin. *Hasta luego.*" The stoplight turned green. Marco's tires screeched and he spun out, stealing a glance back at Eva.

"Seriously, does that attitude actually work with some women?" Eva said.

"Marco is weird, from what I've seen. I mean I've known the guy for years—even before I went into prison. And he seems to have gotten weirder in the last three years—much weirder. Specifically with how he relates to women."

"Does he like the kind of weird stuff we got into on that

first night?" Eva teased, putting her hand back on my shoulder. "Does he, *papi?*"

I smiled and kept my eyes on the road. Although we were just playing, her hand on me felt good. "Christ, Eva, you would play the shit out of this undercover role. If you let yourself get into it and don't hold back."

My phone buzzed in the nook between our seats, and Eva picked it up. "Do you trust me enough to give me your key code?"

"Draw a big square starting in the top left," I said.

"You're not a complicated man, are you?"

"Only when it comes to you. What's it say?" I stole a glance at Eva. Her normally tan face had gone white, the blood run out of it.

"It's from Marco. He says 'Good to see you and your hot piece of ass Alexa. I want to invite both of you to come down to the mansion in Mexico with me. You wanted to meet Luis--so I will introduce you. We leave tonight. Pack light.'"

I pulled up in front of Eva's apartment. "So does this mean that your first undercover role is officially going to be as my sidepiece? Congratulations."

"You know, I'm really starting to come around to getting into the role of Alexa. Just promise me you'll be a good *papi*," she pursed her lips sarcastically in a sexy smile as she got out of the car without directly answering my question.

"So you'll do it?"

The same grin plastered across her face, she shut the door without answering.

I couldn't tell if she seriously liked playing my sidepiece or not. At first, it seemed like the dumbest thing ever to bring Eva undercover with me. But something about her had me thinking she could be the key to the whole operation.

Or maybe I was just looking for another excuse to spend more time with her.

I felt movement between my legs as I watched her walking out of the car toward her apartment.

I knew she could handle herself in danger, but there was this aura of innocence around her that I couldn't quite get over. She had no idea how evil Marco could be, or what she was about to get mixed up with.

14

EVA

I nside my apartment, I immediately went to the bathroom and turned the bathtub faucet on until the water was nice and warm. I let it run while I disrobed and opened a bottle of red wine.

I wasn't usually an afternoon drinker, but today I needed one. I only had two hours left to give Ned my yes or no, and the way my head was still pounding, I could use a little hair of the dog. Wine, a bubble bath, and my favorite Mary J. Blige album would be my counsel.

I eased into the warm water, a faint smile on my face as I leaned my head back, almost resting it on the porcelain of the tub. The red blend felt soothing on my throat.

To go undercover with Corbin, or not to go? That was the question, subconscious, that we were here to debate.

I'd like to call to the stand my first witness. The amazing sex.

Before Corbin and I's romp, it had been months since I'd had any at all. It might have even been *years* since I'd had sex like *that*. I'd even surprised myself with how good it was. I'd never been a one night stand kind of girl—in the past I'd always thrived on an emotional connection with my partners. Yet with Corbin, it'd been different. Sexy, physical, and orgasmic. The chemistry was palpable, even though I couldn't exactly explain why.

It wasn't that sex with Ned had been *bad*. Who complains about sex anyway? Sex is like pizza. Even when it was bad, it was still pretty good.

Right?

Sex with Ned had been...*nice.* Just like most things with Ned, until we broke it off. He was a *nice* man who did *nice* things for me and made love almost in a reserved, *obligatory* way. As a result, I was underwhelmed throughout the relationship—only just now was I piecing together what I was missing.

Listening to Mary J Blige made me think back to the nineties and the music I grew up with. I liked to think it was the last early hip hop era, the golden era before music went soft. For some reason, I thought about the rap I used to listen to and a Jay-Z lyric stuck out in my head: *It's kind of hard to go back to hamburger helper after you've had that filet mignon.*

What song was that lyric from? Did it matter? I sank further into the bubble bath, sticking my toes out of the water.

Take the job, my first witness said. *Take the job and stop being so worried about what other people think about you. You're too damn NICE, Eva.*

I nodded at my thought, and I had to laugh. Did other people have conversations with themselves like I did?

I called my second witness to the stand, career progress.

I'll be short, this witness said.

You damn well know you need to accept this job and go undercover. When else are you going to get an opportunity to take down a man as villainous as Reyes? If you don't seize this opportunity, you're going to end up pushing papers in ten years, at the same desk, and you're going to be very pissed. Stop being so damn NICE and go after what YOU want for a change.

Career was right. Corbin out of the picture, I *did* want this job. I'd been wanting to go into the field ever since I found out how my cousin was gunned down, caught in the crossfire of senseless gun violence.

Plus, Corbin is so damn sexy, if you go undercover with him maybe you'll...

My witnesses were starting to get a little bit out of control. *Sex, pipe down. You've already taken the stand.*

The Mary J Blige track "I'm goin' down" played in the background, and I took another sip of my wine. I let her lyrics sound through me as I meditated.

I leaned back in the water and let my whole body submerge except for my face.

Both of the witnesses *Sex* and *Career* seemed to agree, but for different reasons. I knew what I had to do. There would be no more *Little Miss Nice Girl.* I had been running scared for far too long, afraid to take my career to the next level. It was time for me to do what it took to win, and I would start with my career. And although *Sex* made a strong case, I'd have to take sex with Corbin off the table for my own piece of mind. It was just a complication that I didn't need.

I rose up out of the water, and fired off some texts.

Eva: I'm going to do this mission with you, I've decided

Corbin: Yes! More time with the prettiest girl I've ever met

Eva: But...

Corbin: Not a but. I don't like buts. Unless we're talking about your butt

Eva: I'm serious. No sex on this trip. And I mean it. You're great and all but when we're out of the Reyes' sight, we drop the roles. Capiche?

Corbin: (two baseball emojis)

Eva: What does that mean?

Corbin: Can we at least round second base?

My phone buzzed suddenly, and I took a deep breath when I saw it was my brother Jake calling. I blew out the air and composed myself.

"Speak of the devil! I was just about to give you a call."

"Oh yeah?" Jake replied. "Your ears were burning?"

I smiled. "Yes. I'm trying to make a difficult decision. Can I get your advice?"

"Of course."

"If you had to do something really difficult...and it could end up being the best thing you ever did, but it could blow up in your face times one-hundred, what would you do?"

He paused for a moment. "Wow. Getting right down to business tonight, aren't we."

"I didn't mean to bombard you. If you don't want to answer..."

"Well what's the opportunity?"

"I can't say."

"Ohh..it's classified?"

"I can neither agree nor disagree with that statement."

Jake chuckled. "Of course. My advice? All the good things in life come hard. And even if something good comes easy, we don't appreciate it as much. So if I were you, I'd go for it, one-hundred percent. So you really can't tell me?"

"I can't."

He sighed. "Alright I guess...I'm just a little worried about you. That's all."

"You didn't call to give me a free counseling session. What did you call for?"

He laughed, and I could see that boyish smile forming on his face, even through the phone.

"I'm getting married."

I choked on the air, cleared my throat, and then coughed some more. "Excuse me?"

"I said I--"

"I understood the words! Is this a trick?"

He chuckled again. "Not a trick."

"Jake, the last time we spoke your position on marriage wasn't exactly...favorable."

"Oh you mean when I'd sworn off the *idea* of considering the idea of marriage? Well, that was post-break up Jake. New Jake has a new girl...and she's incredible."

"What the...I haven't even met her yet."

"Well you should come to Chicago soon and meet her. She's amazing. Deal?"

"Deal. Wow. Lot of ladies are going to be disappointed that the bad boy of baseball has finally settled down."

"They'll live."

I glanced at the time. "Oh, damn, Jake I have to go. I'll look for the details in the mail. Bye bro, I love you."

"Bye Eva. I know you'll make the right decision, whatever you decide."

I hung up the phone with a new resolve, knowing exactly what it was I had to do.

THE AFTERNOON LIGHT sneaked into Ned's office as he paced around the room, tie half undone, sweating up a storm as usual. I sat on the two-seater couch with my legs crossed. Corbin picked up a bowl of pistachios from Ned's coffee table and sifted through them, looking for the easiest ones to eat as Ned reacted to our plan.

"I don't feel comfortable with this, Eva. You want to go undercover as Corbin's arm candy, his *mistress*? How did you come up with this plan, anyway? I can't in good faith approve this mission. What if you have to, you know, *do stuff*?" Ned shook his head vigorously.

I furrowed my brow. What were we, in sixth grade? "Do *stuff*? It's an unorthodox plan, but we need to be unorthodox to catch Luis Reyes. That's exactly why he won't suspect it. And yeah, we might have to lay a couple of kisses on each other. I promise I won't use any tongue, though," I winked.

Corbin chimed in. "If you have a better idea, Ned, I'm all ears. I, for one, think we should consider ourselves lucky to have a woman like Eva who fits the bill for my sidepiece and can play the part convincingly." He cocked his head at me and winked.

Ned did a double take at the word *sidepiece*, and loosened his tie further. I had a feeling he had a personal reason for resisting this plan.

"And how on earth do you know she can play it convincingly? Eva is a *nice* girl, Corbin. I have my doubts she can act as badly as she'll need to."

My heart recoiled when Ned said the words *nice girl*. This was precisely the image I was trying to correct. How could I correct it without compensating too far in the 'bitchy slut' direction? It was a fine line I had to walk.

Ned loosened his tie and looked back and forth between the two of us, shaking his head. "Fucking great. Jesus. Just what I need: a goddamn vigilante squad. What a dynamic fucking duo! Our ex-con superstar and my first time field agent coming up with their own ideas. I thought Eva being Corbin's long lost cousin was a splendid idea."

Ned turned his back to look out the window for a moment, and Corbin and I exchanged a look. He stuck his tongue out and mouthed the words *you're hot*.

"Fine," Ned finally said. "You've convinced me. Damned if it's not the craziest plan I've ever heard, but shit, you're right Eva. We need to be unorthodox to catch Reyes." He ambled over behind his desk, opened a drawer, and pulled out a tiny electronic chip, barely the size of his thumbnail.

"This," Ned said, "is your lifeblood. It's a voice transmitter, recorder, and GPS tracker all in one once we activate it. This baby is how we are going catch him. It's what we will use in trial once we finally have the bastard extradited." He held it up to the light.

"It looks easy to lose," Corbin said. "Not to mention, Marco is going to be suspicious if we have a tiny piece of amazing technology."

Ned reached in his desk and pulled out a rubik's cube. "We'll hide it in this. Middle yellow square." He popped off the yellow tab of the cube, hid the chip inside it, and replaced the tab. He spun it a few times and it certainly looked just like a normal rubik's cube again.

Ned walked around his desk until he was right in front of Corbin. "Listen. You take care of her, okay?" he put the rubik's cube in Corbin's hand.

"I like puzzles," Corbin says, picking up the cube and spinning it a few times. "Shouldn't be too hard to keep an eye on."

"I'm not talking about the damn rubik's cube, Corbin. I'm talking about my agent," he motioned toward me. "And document everything with that cube. I want Luis Reyes recorded talking about the millions of dollars he's made selling cocaine. I want hard fucking evidence."

I stood. "We're cutting it close. Marco wants to meet us in a couple of hours, and I don't even have my bags packed."

I needed to work on my skanky girl wardrobe, which was seriously lacking.

Ned nodded. I walked out and Corbin followed, rubik's cube in hand.

"Let's do this shit, *Alexa,*" he said close behind me.

A surge of adrenaline ran through me. I liked it when Corbin called me that.

15

CORBIN

Eva sat next to me in the cab on the way to the meetup site with Marco. Her hair blew in the wind like she was a puppy looking out the window. For our border crossing, she had donned denim short shorts and a black spaghetti strap tank top. I could hardly believe I was looking at the same woman that I saw in the office earlier today in slacks and a blazer. I couldn't get over her ability to vacillate between being the kind of woman you'd be scared to confront in the boardroom to the woman that you would want to grind on late at night at the club to some cumbia beats while you felt her flesh up against you.

I held the rubik's cube in my hand, very aware that all of our conversations from here on out would be recorded under the watchful ears of Ned and his team. Not that I cared if Ned or anyone else heard us fucking like rabbits, which I was pretty sure we might have to do.

Anything other than that would make Marco suspicious. And I *knew* he'd be watching us somehow since we were going to be on his turf at the mansion.

"So is this pretty much your fantasy weekend?" she

whispered so the cab driver couldn't hear. We never knew who might be an informant for Marco. "You get to bring me across the border to Mexico and dominate me, eh?"

I smiled. "Are you saying you're *not* going to love being my mistress for a few days? Secretly, of course. You don't have to admit it to any of your friends," I teased.

"Oh yes! That's what I've always wanted to be. How about we start things off on the right foot. Make sure we're in character."

"What do you mean?"

Eva took off her seatbelt and straddled my lap. She ran her hand along my tattooed bicep down to my forearm. "I mean we should arrive to this airfield showing Marco what a great little *mami* I am for my *papi.*"

"Eva—"

She slapped my cheek and grabs my jaw. "There is no more Eva. Only *Alexa.*" She whispered in my ear and bit slightly on my lobe. My cock simmered beneath her.

"Fuck yes. I like Alexa," I said as she ran her hand up and down my chest. She let her mouth hang half open, her luscious red lips tempting me. She kissed me on the cheek.

"Awwww. Is my *papi* getting *duro?*"

Eva pressed her cheek against mine and put a hand on my abs, poking a delicate finger under my pants and belt.

"You're so sexy, *papi,*" she whispered again in my ear. "Mmm, I love it when you get all worked up."

"No one gets me as worked up as you do," I growled.

The cab driver slammed on the brakes, jerking Eva from her position on top of me.

"We're here," he said.

There was a rap on the window and I lowered it. It was Marco, staring at us with a gun in his hands.

"Nice to see your girl is taking care of you," he said, glancing at Eva with a dark smile.

Eva swallowed. I shot her a look that said *relax, we're fine* as Marco opened the door and we were met by the cool night air. We were at the outskirts of town now, and could see a few more stars than we could in the city of San Diego. A couple of thuggish looking men in tattoos stood behind Marco with their arms crossed.

"These are Hugo and Pablo," Marco said, nodding toward them.

"You expecting a fight sometime soon?" I asked.

"When visiting a man like Luis Reyes, you can never be too sure who you'll meet en route," Marco answered with a wry smile. "Now, I hope you two don't mind. It's not that I don't trust you, but..." he snapped his finger and nodded at the two men, who proceeded to give us each a personal pat-down from head to toe. They also unzipped our bags and Eva's purse and rifled through them.

"Is this how you treat all of your respected guests?" I said and stretched my arms over my head. "I thought the purpose of this trip was to talk about a partnership."

"Of course it is," Marco says. "And trust, me, there is no one I should trust more. But you know how it is in this business. Luis Reyes is a man of extreme precaution, even with his friends."

"With enemies like that..." Eva chimed in.

"Does your woman always talk this much?" Marco cut her off.

"She has a bad habit of speaking," I smirked. Eva didn't flinch.

Marco's man finished patting me down. "He's clean, boss."

The man who had patted down Eva nodded as well. Not

like she had a whole lot of places to check in those tight-ass jeans.

"*Bueno*," Marco said. "Let's board the plane." He gestured to a large black Hummer parked in the lot.

"Perfect. Where does the plane take off from?" I asked.

"From here," Marco said. "We've nicknamed our Hummer *The Plane*. I hope it's not too confusing for you. But it helps to confuse the authorities. They'll intercept real texts and conversations about a 'plane' and spend the next 48 hours monitoring the border air traffic. Meanwhile, we're gone, on the ground. It's quite genius, actually." He gestured to his bodyguards, and they pick up Eva's and my bags. "Shall we?"

I nodded and walked toward the vehicle.

"After you, *mi amor*," Marco said, waiting for Eva to pass. "I'll bring up the rear if you don't mind."

Marco stared at Eva as she walked toward the van. He surveyed her body up and down and smiled ever so slightly at her. I'd been acquainted with Marco long enough to know that he was like a little kid when it came to women: he coveted the ones he couldn't have, and that's exactly what he was doing at this precise moment: coveting Eva.

I locked eyes with Eva for a moment when I helped her into the Hummer. If she was nervous, she hid it well. I was about to follow her into the vehicle when Marco stopped me by grabbing my arm.

"Alexa is incredible. I even love the way she walks," he said. "You simply *must* let me try her during your visit." Marco scratched his head with the nozzle of his old fashioned gun, a colt forty-five.

"I'll think about it. I've been keeping her pretty busy."

"I see. Well, for now, I'll settle for just sitting in the back with her. Why don't you have a seat with the girl I've brought for the night, Louisa."

Fuck if I was letting Marco chat with Eva for the whole ride.

"I think the men should sit in back. Talk business. Leave the whores up front."

Marco thought about it for a second. "Yes, that's good. Alexa, sit in the front with Louisa."

She hopped in, flashing a devilishly sexy smile at Marco and I.

This was going to be tougher than I thought. Finding Luis Reyes—that would be the easy part. The difficult part was going to be making sure Marco left her the fuck alone.

I had to make sure he knew she was mine and only mine.

16

EVA

The Hummer took us southeast, away from San Diego and toward Mexico's Baja desert. To avoid a checkup by border patrol, we drove under a tunnel that started a mile or so out from the great wall that separated Mexico and the U.S. My heartbeat accelerated as we drove into the darkness through the bumpy road. I'd never liked closed spaces, and this was no exception.

Whatever Corbin was saying to Marco in the back, they were laughing raucously. Corbin had a knack for acting like an asshole and fitting right in with these guys. Sometimes, I got this feeling that I was the one who was having the wool pulled over my eyes, not Marco. Whenever I asked him what they were talking about, Marco or Corbin simply would say "man talk, honeybuns," and then crack up like a couple of middle-schoolers who had just made a 'cooties' joke.

While the boys were in the back, I was sitting captain next to Marco's girl Louisa. She wore a tight little tube top dress, her voluptuous breasts nearly pouring out the top of them. I couldn't tell if those were a gift from God or a gift from Marco and a really good plastic surgeon. My instinct said it was probably the latter. I took it upon myself to get all of the information I could from her.

"I like your dress," I smiled and touched Louisa's arm.

"Thanks, Marco got it for me," she said, her eyes lighting up.

"How long have you and Marco been...you know. Hanging out."

"You mean working together? A couple of months," she averted her eyes away from mine and brushed her pretty blonde hair behind her ear.

I leaned in closer to her and whispered, not wanting the armed guard in the seat in front to be able to hear me.

"Do you enjoy working for him?"

"He's really not so bad. He has strange tastes, that's for sure, but who doesn't?"

Strange tastes. I want so badly to ask her to elaborate, but I opted to do my job and play the role conservatively, without prying too much. Seemed like a good idea given I could tell the guy in the front seat was eavesdropping on our conversation.

"Yeah, Corbin's into some weird stuff too," I agreed with her.

She smiled faintly, almost fakely, and I mirrored her. "What's that?" she asked, pointing to the rubik's cube sticking out of my handbag.

Uh oh. That should have been a little deeper in my bag.

"Oh, that? It's nothing."

She continued, plowing through my hesitation. "I've seen those before. It's a fun cube. You mind if I play with it?"

She just called a Rubik's cube a fun cube. That's a first. "Well, I guess."

I glanced around the vehicle to see if anyone was

watching me. All the men were engaged in their own conversations. I handed her the cube.

"Just make sure you give it back."

WE DROVE FURTHER INTO MEXICO, into the heart of the Reyes operation. I stared out the window into the blackness. Northern Mexico had some of the most evil and vicious gangs in the entire world. Lately, the murder rates in some areas had been enough to elevate them to 'warzone' status. Such a sad state of affairs.

As I gazed out at the Mexican countryside, I found myself fantasizing about the electricity that flowed through my body the last time I was in Mexico.

I felt an element of pure honesty that first night between Corbin and I. Even if I wasn't telling him my real name, I just felt he *got me*. When he looked in my eyes and smiled at me, it was like he knew me inside and out. We were just two messed up souls united in our craziness, our faults.

It was funny that riding in the car as Corbin's mistress in ridiculous short shorts and a top that I hadn't worn for years, I felt more at ease with myself than I had in a long time. I looked back at Corbin. He and Marco were both staring at me. Corbin blew me an exaggerated kiss, and he and Marco laughed.

A smile slowly spread across my face. I couldn't believe I was thinking this, but Corbin's assholery was actually starting to grow on me. In the heat of the most critical mission of my life, I didn't even feel alarmed. I felt at ease. I wasn't sure if that was a good thing or a bad thing.

The vehicle came to a halt in front of a gate. The armed guard in the passenger's seat opened his window and said some words in Spanish to another man with a gun, and the gate opened.

"We have arrived," Marco announced, leaning his head forward into the captain's chairs. He looked inquisitively at Louisa, who had made quick progress on the rubik's cube. She made a few more turns on it and locked it into place.

"Done!" She said, and turned to me like a grade school student who had just finished their homework early, extending her arm out with the toy.

Marco didn't smile. "What is this?" he asked, snatching it from her hand.

"It's a rubik's cube," I said. "It's a puzzle. You try to get all of the sides to be the same—"

"I know what a goddamn rubik's cube is," Marco cut me off. "Why do you have this?"

"Roadtrip game," I said.

Marco looked back at Corbin. "Smart fucking girl you've got here. Playing games like this."

"She wasn't the one who solved it though," Corbin pointed out. "Looks like Louisa's smarter."

Louisa looked down sheepishly. Inside, I couldn't believe they were arguing over whose girl was dumber like it was some kind of accomplishment. Outside, I wore my plastic smile.

"I guess you're right. I think I'll hang onto this cube. I've never solved one of these, and I'd very much like to try. Thanks."

Marco gave the cube a couple of spins before he tucked it into his pocket. His lips curled up in a sinister expression that I couldn't quite call a smile. He stroked the sides of his mustache with his right finger and thumb. My heart pounded like a steel drum. Corbin shot me a *you had one job* look from the back.

I wanted to tell him, that yes, I had one job—to get that rubik's cube close to Marco and Luis Reyes. Mission accomplished.

"Welcome to the Reyes mansion. Consider yourselves lucky. Not many people get to see it and..." he trailed off for a moment.

And what? I wanted to say. *And live?* Marco trailed off and sort of looked out the window.

"...And it's very big."

"That's what she said," I uttered, and as soon as I said it, I covered my mouth. That was entirely an Eva joke, not something Alexa would say. Marco narrowed his eyes at me and luckily, chuckled.

"That girl of yours, she's got *some* lip. I find it amusing."

The guard opened the door and Louisa stepped out, long legs first.

"She does have nice lips on her. I like a little sass, though. Sass and ass, the two best qualities a woman can have." Corbin looked at me as we got ready to step onto the ground and head into the infamous Reyes mansion.

"What are you waiting for, Alexa?" Corbin said. "Ladies first."

17

CORBIN

"Corbin, your room will be upstairs," Marco said as we walked from the SUV to the front door of the Reyes mansion. "And Alexa, yours will be—"

"Alexa and I will stay in the same room," I cut him off.

"You prefer to sleep in the same bed as your whore?" he asked. "Interesting."

I couldn't quite make out Marco's expression in the moonlight, but he seemed slightly irritated. Knowing him, he was probably planning on making a stealth move to Eva's room later that night, and no way in hell was I allowing that to happen.

"Well I sure as hell didn't bring this hot piece of ass here just to look at. Although the view *is* nice," I smirked and noticed Marco's glance drifting to Eva as she walked in front of us. His eyes lingered on her beautiful figure, and I couldn't say I blamed him for looking considering how hot she was in her little denim short shorts.

As we entered the house, I slipped my hand down to the small of Eva's back. Marco's gaze drifted to my hand. A porter entered the house, carrying our bags. He walked past us and started up the stairs.

"Good night then, Marco," I said. "It's late. We'll talk business tomorrow. Will Luis be here?"

"We will see, cabrón Corbin. Get some rest," Marco returned, and I noted that he did not directly answer my question.

"Goodnight Marco," Eva added in a sing-song tone.

"Goodnight Alexa," Marco said, with much more enthusiasm than he had spoken the words to me.

We followed the porter and maid upstairs to our room. It was spacious—as big as the suites I had stayed at in Las Vegas. He opened up the sliding door to the balcony outside, and the crisp night air streamed in. The maid showed us the bathroom, living room, and hot tub on the balcony. "Guest room" was an understatement. This was excess at its finest. Luis Reyes surely had created this room for the express purpose of impressing his honored, high rolling drug-dealing guests staying here.

And, I for one, was decently fucking impressed. Incredible what drug money would buy.

The maid left and the porter closed the door, finally leaving Eva and I alone. She took off her earrings and placed them on top of the dresser. I walked over to her and put my hands on her shoulders, slipping my fingers under her black spaghetti strap. I gave her a light massage for a minute or so. She didn't say anything. She just breathed deeply.

While my thumbs made slow circles on her back and neck, I looked around the room once more. What I saw in the corner opposite us in the ceiling set alarm bells off in my head.

A camera. He set up a goddamn camera in here.

The fucking voyeur. I hadn't met Luis Reyes, but I already didn't like him. And I wouldn't doubt that he'd given Marco access to that footage as well. We could not fall out of our roles, even when we were alone in our own room.

This was going to make things interesting.

Eva took hold of my hands and spun around to face me.

"So, *cabrón Corbin,*" she said, speaking the words with her perfect accent. "You know what we agreed on. When we're alone you can't be touching—"

"It's hot," I cut her off. "We should shower off before bed."

"We should?" she raised her eyebrows.

"Yes, we *should,*" I said emphatically, leaving no room for argument.

Being out of character with a camera pointing right at me could spell a quick end to our plan, and our lives, so I took her by the hand and led her to the bathroom. While I waited for the water to heat up, I took off my shirt.

Eva crossed her arms. "Corbin, out there I don't care how much of an asshole you want to be, but when we are alone you don't have to—" I wrapped my arms around her and covered her mouth with mine. There she went with that damn sass again. She held out her arms away from me, refusing to even touch me with them before pushing me off her.

"What are you doing?" she said sternly.

"Shhhh," I said, taking off my boxers. "I need you to trust me."

"Fine. You want to do this? You want it your way?" She rolled her eyes and started to wiggle her way out of those tight denim shorts.

I stepped into the shower and inspected the walls, which

were an old fashioned design made up of alternating blue and white tile. I found it highly unlikely Luis had bugged the shower, unless he was the most paranoid guy on the face of the earth. I had to duck down under the shower rack, as the plumbing in this mansion was clearly not made for anyone over six feet tall like me.

Eva disrobed in a hurry. Seeing her naked skin made my cock twitch. *Not this time big guy.* I sent him thoughts of sports and teletubbies, the most non-sexual things I could think of.

Eva reluctantly stepped in the shower and joined me, her frown denoting that she was ready to slap me.

She leaned in and I took the opportunity to whisper loudly in her ear. "Eva, there is a camera above the bed. The room is bugged. We cannot fall out of character." Her eyes narrowed and I saw the wheels turning. We switched places so she was under the water, and I feigned needing to lather myself with some soap.

"And the shower is probably the only place we can talk safely," Eva finished my thought.

"Exactly."

"So you don't want to fuck me in the shower."

The way she said the words, I thought I sensed a slight bit of disappointment. I smirked a little. Not like the thought hadn't entered my mind.

"That's not what I'm thinking about right now. Although I do think it would be a good idea to make some skin slap-ping noises and some grunts in here, just to cover our bases. You know, stuff that could be picked up outside."

She held onto my shoulder and got onto her tippy toes to speak directly into my ear, her soft, wet flesh pushing into my body. "You think Marco will actually be listening to us?"

"I've known Marco a long time, and the guy is a freak," I

said. "It wouldn't surprise me at all if he is getting his kicks watching a sex tape of us."

"I mean his mustache is pretty fucking weird. And the way he's always looking at me..."

"Exactly. He's like a lot of guys with access to unlimited money with a lot of power—the only things that turn him on anymore are those things he can't have. And since you're with me, he can't have you. And it's driving him crazy. You can see it in his eyes."

I switched places again with Eva. This time our bodies rubbed against each other and she grabbed hold of my hip, then rubbed her wet upper thigh between my legs.

"Hey, what the hell are you doing?" I asked.

"Keeping my balance," she answered coyly, flashing a flirty smile at me.

Those eyes. Fuck.

"You better keep your hands off me or you're asking for it."

She smiled. "For what?"

"Nothing," I said, doing my best to ignore the fact that most of my blood was flowing directly to my penis. Maybe she wouldn't notice.

She glanced down between my legs. I was wrong.

"That's all it takes? Just me grazing your hip? You're like a teenaged boy for God's sake."

"Around you, I am. But we're not doing this, don't worry. I just have to work a little penis voodoo."

I concentrated on thinking of anything besides Eva's gorgeous, voluptuous body in front of me, her entire body soaking wet. She had one hand on her big, round breasts just on the bottom border of my peripheral vision. Her wet blonde hair fell behind her head like this was some stupid rom-com and we were in the rain, waiting for our first kiss.

The difference was I knew exactly what kissing Eva felt like. Hell, I knew what *everything* felt like. That was definitely not rom-com sex we had one month ago.

I needed to be thinking of anything else besides Eva. But I couldn't. It was hard. It was fucking hard.

And yes, *it* was fucking hard, too.

"Well, it appears we have a big problem here, don't we," she smiled, amused at my failed attempt to make my erection go away.

"Ah, just give me a few minutes to meditate...or something." I'd never meditated. I had no idea why I said that.

"I've been thinking. We had better put on a show for Marco when we get out there." She wiggled her eyebrows. "Just kissing, that's it."

"Good idea. Just kissing? Maybe we should buck a little bit to make sure it's convincing. You know, grind our bodies together and make some ooh's and aah's."

"I'm quite good at faking orgasms. I did it for years with my ex."

"Perfect. I bet you've been dying to put that skill set to good use, and now you can. Just be warned, I'm not going to go easy on you with this fake sex."

"I wouldn't want you to," she batted her eyes at me.

"Oh and *Alexa*," I ran my hand through her thick, wet hair. "The minute I turn this shower head off, you don't break character. Not for a second."

"Don't worry, *papi*," she said. "If it's a show Marco wants, a show he'll get."

We locked eyes, and for a split second, I forgot everything. I forgot I was in Mexico, only here to get out of serving a jail sentence. For a moment, there was just Eva and I.

I turned the water off and took a deep breath.

In that moment, I wanted her more than I'd ever wanted a woman before.

18

EVA

Corbin and I laid on our sides in bed, our faces inches from each other.

Naked except for my bra.

I could feel the heat of his body radiating from his skin even though we weren't quite touching. Like a game of chicken, we both refused to make the first move. Or should I say the first *fake* move.

Maybe Corbin was just teasing me. But he definitely wasn't the shy type.

Out of the corner of my eye I saw the camera in the room, and I did my best to remind myself that this was for show.

We were behind enemy lines, and if Luis Reyes suspected even for a second that something was off between the sexual dynamic of Corbin and I, that could mean death for us.

So we needed to make this convincing.

My heart palpitated as our lips drew closer together so we were just millimeters apart. He put his hand on my hip and brought my body into his. I closed my eyes and felt Corbin's lips finally eclipse the remaining space between us as I breathed heavily.

A wave of electricity pumped through my body. He grazed my neck and back lightly with his fingers. I brought my hand around his head, and ran my fingers through his thick brown hair.

Uh oh. Houston, we have a problem.

I wanted Corbin. *Bad.*

And I didn't want to just dry hump him for the cameras under the covers like we were in a high school play together. *Wait, what kind of high school play lets its students dry hump?* The logical half of my brain had totally stopped functioning.

I wanted to feel him just like the first night.

We kissed sweetly and slowly this time. I didn't recall Corbin being such a good kisser from our one night stand. Maybe that was because I was too concentrated on how many *O's* I was having to think about the kissing.

I did my best to stop thinking about Corbin and how much I wanted him to take me, the real me, Eva. *Don't think about Corbin's muscular arms wrapped around you*, it said. *Don't think about how such a strong and powerful man is touching you so lightly and carefully with his fingertips.* And for God's sake, *do not think about the big cock that is stiffening and touching your thigh.*

My self-talk wasn't working. At all. Clearly I needed a new strategy.

Corbin's tongue ran over the outline of my lips and I battled his mouth with mine. I grabbed a tussle of Corbin's hair. He responded to my touch by wrapping his arm around my middle. Pulling our hips together, he let out a low throaty growl. A shiver started in my heart and ran from my head to my toes.

Resistance was futile. I kept getting wetter by the second.

"Corbin," I let out a long, low whisper. Corbin opened his eyes.

"Yes?"

"I want you."

"You're doing a damn fine job right now," he smiled and whispered in my ear. "Oscar worthy." He lightly bit my lobe. I could hear him breathing and feel the heat coming off his face.

"No. *Really.*"

Corbin squinted, as if he was deciding if I was just acting really well, or if I was serious about breaking my pact of no sex. I arched my back and moaned. My earlobe was one of my spots, and Corbin was breaking me down.

I tried in vain to convince myself this was still about the undercover mission.

It's not real. We're faking it.

The wet spot between my legs was as real as it got.

It's just a game.

If the weight of Corbin's muscular body on top of mine was a game, it was the most fun game I'd ever played.

His mouth smashed mine and I closed my eyes, forgetting where I was. I reached my arms up to the headboard and let his nimble hands work behind my back to unhook my bra. I arched my back, and Corbin took this as an invitation to work his way down my face, neck and chest with his tongue.

"Just do it," I said.

He raised an eyebrow and floated his face back up above mine, hovering over me and leaning on one of his arms. A strategic hand stayed behind, rubbing my thigh.

"You want me to...go down on you?" he whispered in my ear. "I'm sorry, Eva, I just can't. I think we were pretty clear on the rules. *You* were pretty clear on the boundaries you wanted to set."

"I want you. I need you," I moaned and ran my hand along the back of his muscular thigh. "Stop playing."

"Oh, are we done playing?"

Corbin smirked and began to move his body to one side to hop off me. Instinctively, I reached up to grab his hip and stopped him from getting away. My hand, however, accidently grabbed his junk.

"Jesus Corbin, you are hard as a rock," I murmured, surprised at how engorged he was.

Corbin let out a throaty breath. "What are you doing, baby?" he looked down in an opiatic stare, his eyes glazed over.

I couldn't take it anymore. I was done letting him tease me.

"Please, Corbin. I want you to fuck me."

I batted my eyes to make sure he knew there was no sarcasm to that comment.

"Touché," Corbin said.

He wrapped his arms around my legs and dragged me to the edge of the bed so my butt was almost hanging off it, my feet pointing straight up in the air. He knelt on the floor so his face was at the perfect level for what he was about to do.

Corbin looked up at me with his lips curved upward in a smirk. "If this is a game, I think I like this game." He licked around my legs, teasing me before he dove between my legs. I curled my fingers into the sheets feeling fire and ice run through me at once.

My eyes wandered to the corner of the room and I again noticed the camera that was pointed directly at us. *Enjoy the show, Marco.* I smiled, as Corbin tongued between my legs, making me twist and turn.

It was a show all right, but there wasn't a thing fake about this anymore. It was ironic that I had spent a whole relationship faking my way through it, pretending everything was fine when it wasn't, and now with Corbin in a fake situation I felt bowled over by how viscerally and truly I wanted this man.

"Corbin, that's enough toying with me," I ran my hand through his thick brown hair. Still kneeling, he glanced up at me. "I want you inside me," I whispered.

I didn't have to tell him twice. Corbin stood up, and my eyes traced the "V" of his chest until they arrived between his legs. He was hard, and still dangling so *low*. If I hadn't already had that thing inside me, I'd wonder if it would even—

"It will fit, stop acting like we haven't already done this," Corbin smirked. "Besides, you are as wet as the Gulf of Mexico right now."

I smiled, fixating on him—not just his manhood, but everything about him at that moment. My eyes jumped from body part to body part. For some reason I was avoiding his gaze.

"Alexa, look at my eyes," he said, staring at me.

A soft smile ran across my face—so much dopamine and oxytocin running through my body. He reached down and put a curled finger underneath my chin, angling my head up and forcing me to stop averting my eyes.

"Alexa, up here. Eyes are up here," he joked again.

"I know exactly where your eyes are. But it's not your eyes I want in me right now."

"You are so impatient sometimes, you know that?"

He turned around, grabbed a golden foil pack from the

dresser and rolled on the condom. He climbed back on the bed and knelt in front of me, still not entering me yet.

"Let me give you a hand," I said. I reached down and grabbed hold of his girth with two hands and guided it between my legs.

"Fuck, Alexa," he groaned. He slid in slowly, one inch at a time. I turned my head to the side and stifled a moan in the pillow.

Corbin teased me with shallow strokes.

"You sure you want it?"

"Yes."

"Are you sure?"

"Stop fucking with me and fuck me already," I said. "Please."

He smiled and gave in to my demand, pushing all the way in. Feeling suddenly full, I let out a whimper.

"It's okay," he whispered, guiding my face toward his. "You can scream as loud as you want here."

He grabbed hold of my hips with one hand and my head with the other as he stroked back and forth. I ground my hips against him in rhythm.

"Mmmhmmm," was all I managed to get out between moans.

"It's so hot when you moan like that," Corbin said.

The thought that I was turning him on made me moan louder.

For a moment, he paused. "Don't stop," I said, perhaps even a tinge of annoyance in my voice when he slowed down.

We bucked together, he grabbed onto my hair and pinned me down, forcing me to stare into his icy blue eyes. I moaned as the pleasure came in waves. I loved the feel of his big body on top of me, taking me how he wanted.

"Let's change positions," he said.

"Take me however you want."

He pulled out for a moment and angled my legs toward the ceiling, pushing my knees toward me like the happy baby yoga position. My legs together, I felt him squeeze inside me.

Remember that other *spot*? Nope, I realized I was wrong. *This* was *the spot*.

Corbin was carrying me away to the third layer of heaven. As he plunged into me again and again, I didn't stifle my moans. Instead, I embraced them.

"Harder, Corbin," I moaned.

I felt his hips hitting mine with every stroke. I clenched around him, he felt so big and hard.

"Deeper," I commanded. I had been staring at Corbin's chest, and I looked up at his eyes to find him staring right back at me as I felt his thrusts somehow go further inside me. We were both alone in our own worlds of pleasure, but we were both somehow together too.

"You're going to come, aren't you?" Corbin growled.

"Ughn hun," I managed to squeak.

"Do it. Come for me, baby."

I was wordless as I arched my back, reached my hands out and grasped at Corbin—grasped at anything in the vicinity. I wanted an anchor to hold as I let go completely. I felt like I might just float away.

We bucked like wild animals. I shook, and when the thunder between us finally subsided, I opened my eyes and saw his sweaty face, inches from mine.

"God it's so hot when you writhe like that," Corbin said as I floated back to reality, calming my breath. He stayed inside me a moment before he pulled out, and I groaned at the empty feeling he left me with.

"It's easy when you're doing...what you do," I mouthed.

And that's when I realized I was in trouble.

Because rule number one of undercover missions is don't get feelings for your partner.

It's in the handbook. Trust me.

19

CORBIN

The next morning, Eva showered, and I headed downstairs and slipped outside to the patio.

Marco was seated at a table outside with Louisa, and I took a seat across from him.

"*Buenos días,*" I said, my voice gravelly.

"Wish I could have woken up as happy as you did," Marco said, taking a sip of his coffee and shooting me a curious smirk.

"Come again?" I furrowed my brow.

"We could hear you and Alexa down here. Shit. You could be heard all over the property."

"I guess we never did close the balcony. My bad," I laughed.

Marco broke into a smile. He reached across the table and put his hand on my shoulder.

"Good to see you are back and operational again, cabrón. The Corbin of old."

"Coffee?" A maid in a blue and white apron asked me in a heavy Spanish accent.

"Yes please," I answered and she filled my cup. I inhaled

the aroma of the strong brown liquid. I motioned to her and she topped it off with cream.

"So when will Luis Reyes be arriving?" I asked.

"Soon," Marco answered from across the table.

"How soon is soon?" I asked, taking a sip of my coffee. It was impossible to see last night when we arrived in the middle of the night, but the lavishness of the Reyes mansion was on display in the morning sunlight. From our position on top of a hill, I could see all manner of wilderness: fruit trees, brush, and rolling hills as far as the eye could see. And the mansion itself was gigantic—the size of a couple of football fields put together.

"You look tired this morning, Corbin," Marco said, changing the subject. The way he smiled at me, I knew he had watched that video from last night. On the table was the rubik's cube. One side was solved, but the other five sides were still a quilt of different colors.

"Well, you know what this fresh air does to the girls. Drives them *loca*," I took another sip of my coffee and Marco stared back at me. "Makes 'em want to stay up all night doing dirty things."

"And what person wouldn't want to do dirty things with you?" Marco said with an even more devilish smirk that gave me a weird vibe.

I recoiled just a tiny bit, but didn't show it.

"Oh, for sure. They all do."

Is Marco hitting on me?

"How much are you paying Alexa for her company, by the way?" he continued.

"The standard rate, a thousand a day or so," I said, making up a price off the top of my head. I made a mental note to let Eva know that price as soon as I had her alone. "Why do you ask?"

"I ask because I'm curious about your arrangement. You said you picked her up at the club...how did you convince her so quickly to drop everything and come with you? Was she a prostitute before?"

Marco picked up the rubik's cube and turned it over, looking for a strategy to make the colors match.

I raked a hand through my hair. I knew what he was getting at. He was kicking himself for not having done the proper background check on Eva before he allowed her to come with us.

Not good.

"Sometimes, you just find the right woman who is open to a paid arrangement," I said, looking over at Louisa, who was quiet as a mouse. "You seem extra curious."

"Indeed, I'm curious. Luis was asking about it. I showed him a picture of her."

"A picture, eh? Where did you get that?"

I was sure the "picture" Marco was referring to was actually the video he had taken in our room last night. I pursed my lips and held my tongue, using all of my self-control not to jump across the table and punch Marco in the face.

In my logical brain, I knew Eva and I were putting on a show last night in bed. But knowing that Marco was sharing our love-making with his dirty cousin just didn't sit right with me.

Marco averted his eyes and looked down at the ground. I focused on the man for a moment. He was in his early thirties, a little overweight, and with a big mustache and untamed facial hair. I sensed a strange vulnerability coming from him, as if in spite of his drug dealing, villainous image, all he'd ever really been looking for was love from a quality girl. And dealing drugs filled that void for him.

"Look, Marco, women are a little like this rubik's cube

here," I picked it up off the table. "They're complex crea-
tures with many different sides to them. Observe."

I spun the cube a few times and looked for the white
cross. "You've got to start small. Don't try to solve the thing
on the first turn."

In a few more spins, I had the white corners. "This
requires time and patience."

Marco watched me closely. After a few more spins, I had
all of the sides crossed. Now I just needed to match the
corners to the sides.

"The thing is, you can solve one side, like you did, but
the key is not to put all of your energy into getting one side,
it is to look at the thing like the different parts of a whole.
And sometimes, you gotta take a loss to that perfect side to
make things work in the future."

In another minute or so I solved the thing completely.
Marco stared in amazement and I handed it back to him.

His amusing smile turned into a frown. "Or perhaps,
Alexa is simply the perfect puzzle, ready to be solved?" he
said. "How much would I have to pay for a night with her,
do you think?"

My adrenaline surged and I stifled a frown. The last
thing I wanted was to make Marco think I actually cared
about Eva.

Which I did.

*What the fuck does Marco not understand about the fact that
Alexa--Eva--is mine?*

Shit, maybe I didn't know what Eva and I were yet, but I
sure as hell knew that whatever we were didn't involve
Marco getting in on the action. It was a strange feeling, this
possessiveness that had taken hold of me. And more so now
after the night we had last night, which I was still trying to
piece together. I was able to fake our time in bed for all of

thirty seconds before my attraction for Eva overwhelmed me and that shit became real. I didn't know if it was real for her, but it was real for me.

I took a deep breath and looked around at all of the fancy, lavish settings that surrounded us. It was like we were in a Pitbull music video for God's sake. I was reminded that money couldn't buy happiness. For all of the millions the Reyes family had made, a cloud of sadness seemed to follow them around. Mo' money, mo' problems was a way of life for them.

In a strange way it made sense that Marco would want Eva, who was precisely the only girl within his reality who was off-limits to him.

I realized I'd been staring off at the clouds for seconds —minutes?

"Corbin? How much for the girl?" Marco squinted. His square face and mustache came back into focus. Whatever number I named, Marco could pay it. Money wasn't even an issue in the slightest. "Just one night."

"Alexa isn't for sale," I quipped.

Marco leaned forward and frowned.

"You're quite protective of her for just your sidepiece. You're not getting attached to her, are you?"

He was mocking me, searching my face for a sign of weakness. Like the great poker player I was, I gave him nothing to work with. Marco kept on staring at me until we were interrupted.

"Hey boys," I heard Eva's sing song voice call out from the sliding glass door that led out to the patio.

My head automatically swung in her direction. Today she had donned a sexy red dress, looking every bit the part of a prostitute. She also looked hot as fuck in the daylight.

I gulped and hoped Marco didn't see how fast I looked her way.

"Interesting," Marco said. I could feel his eyes still burning on the back of my head.

"What's interesting?" Eva asked as she approached us. She brushed an affectionate finger across my shoulders.

"Oh, nothing, nothing at all," Marco answered as Eva sat down next to me. "I think that I've figured out what needs to happen with this Rubik's cube to solve it, that's all."

20

EVA

L ater that day, Marco took us on a tour of the grounds. A few miles away from where we slept, there was an entirely separate mansion. It wasn't quite as big inside, but it had a plethora of rooms in a dorm room style set up for all of the workers who worked at the mansion: everyone from guards to porters and maids staff.

I felt strange and out of place riding over the dirt roads of the Reyes property in a Rolls-Royce convertible. Marco sat in the front seat while Corbin and I rode in the back, the warm afternoon breeze flowing across our faces. Marco's attachment to me was growing, and it showed in how he spoke to me.

"You should be proud, Alexa. You are the first woman I have allowed to come on this tour," Marco turned back with his hand still on the wheel and looked at me in the back seat as I rode, my body pressed up against Corbin. "But I think you'll be good to give the men some motivation," he added.

"Is this where Luis lives?" Corbin asked in an attempt to change the subject.

"Luis lives wherever he chooses," Marco said. I was

curious as to why Marco would give such a non-answer about Luis. "So, Alexa, where are you from?"

"My mother is from Mexico," I began my made up back-story. "We moved to San Diego when I was seven. We lived south of Nogales in a little town called Santa Ana..."

"Santa Ana? You don't say. I'm familiar with it. And your father, where was he from?"

I gulped. I wondered if he'd have the resources to check up on me, find my real name. "He's a gringo," I said.

"Oh," Marco answered. "Well that explains your freckles, doesn't it?"

I blushed.

"So, like mother, like daughter?" Marco asked me.

"Excuse me? I don't understand what you mean?"

I noticed that I was holding on to Corbin's bicep in the back seat like it was an anchor. He felt like one.

"I mean to say that you like gringos, just like your mother," Marco said with a wink. I couldn't tell where he was going with this.

"Aww, are you getting jealous?" I ribbed, reaching forward and rubbing Marco's shoulder. He smiled, one of the only genuine smiles I'd seen him have in the time we'd interacted. "I can give you a little love too, you know."

As soon as the words came out of my mouth, I regretted saying them. I felt Corbin's bicep twitch; he didn't like the thought of my giving Marco love either.

But out here, there was a very real possibility Marco might 'request' me for a night.

And that could get real interesting.

"That's good to hear," Marco said. "Corbin can be a little protective sometimes. Even of his mistresses."

"*Oh Papi,*" I said, putting my hand on Corbin's chest.

"How could you be jealous? You know you're my number one."

"I'm not jealous," Corbin retorted without expression, and I couldn't tell if he genuinely didn't care if I slept with Marco, or if he was just playing along. "Why would I be?"

Marco was still playing with the rubik's cube in one hand as he drove. He had taken quite the attachment to the thing.

"Oh look!" he said, and showed us that he'd made a cross on each side. "I'm finally getting good at this."

He turned around in his seat, handed the rubik's cube to me, and put his hand on my bare knee. I had to resist recoiling at his leathery touch as the car pulled to a halt in front of mansion number two.

"Alexa, I'm having a party for my staff tonight, and I'd like you to attend. I need a gorgeous woman to bartend for the party...and I would just *love* for you to step in and help out Louisa. A pretty girl like you will help keep up the men's morale. It can get lonely here, being so isolated. What do you think, Corbin?"

"I think it sounds like a fantastic idea," he said. "I know all about isolation. Plus, it'll give us some time to talk business tonight."

The two men stared each other down like two alpha mountain lions who knew only one could be king.

"It sounds fun," I murmured. "I have a new dress I've been wanting to try out anyway. I'm sure the men will get a kick out of it."

I snuggled closer to Corbin, and I swear I saw his jaw twitch from the tension.

21

CORBIN

As the sun was setting that night, Marco and I sat down to talk business while the ladies got ready to put on their "bartending show" or whatever the hell they were doing, and then head to the other mansion.

I came down the steps and walked outside to find Marco sitting down at a table with several of his finest servants standing at the ready.

"Hello Corbin," Marco said. "Have a seat."

He had made up a place just for me with all the trappings for a several course meal as well as two giant wine glasses. Marco's was already filled.

The table was long, with enough room for at least 10 people, but it was only going to be Marco and I. There were only two place-settings.

"Luis couldn't make it, I'm assuming?"

"Luis is held up taking care of some business right now. And as you know, he has entrusted me to do his bidding anyhow."

"Of course," I said as I sat down and a servant pushed my seat in.

A server brought the first course for us, a cold gazpacho.

"Enjoy, sir," the server said.

"Shut the fuck up," Marco interjected, scowling at the server suddenly. He turned to me. "One of my pet peeves is when the server tells me to fucking *enjoy* my meal. Why wouldn't I enjoy it? I fucking picked it."

I shrugged. "Personally, I don't really give a shit what a server says to me."

"Exactly," the server said, nodding.

Marco turned back to the server. "Did I ask you to talk?"

"No, sir. I just thought that—"

"Now there you go, talking again. Again, I didn't ask you to talk." Marco rose up from his seat and grabbed hold of a large metal candlestick from the table.

"Please, Sir."

"That wasn't very smart," Marco said with a scowl. He wound up like a baseball batter, and, spilling wax on the ground and on his own shirt, struck the man in the head.

He screamed as he fell, trying to put his arms up to stop the blows. I'd seen shit like this before. Hell, I'd *been* Marco before. Maybe I still *was* Marco. Even though I hadn't killed since before prison, I knew the violence and the evil lived inside me.

For a moment he paused. "See everybody? This is what happens to people who disobey my instructions." Marco bellowed.

Marco continued striking down blows on the man's head until it turned bloody and his body went limp while his other servants looked on in horror. I knew the feeling that was surging through Marco's veins. There was an extreme power in taking a life—or getting close to it. I wasn't sure if this man was fully dead yet, but he'd certainly need life support after this beating. "Do not fuck with Marco fucking

Reyes," he yelled, and wiped the man's blood from his own forehead.

In the end, the drug world was a wilderness. Kill—exert your power—or risk being seen as weak and get taken advantage of. There was no middle ground. Kill or be killed.

And Marco's over-the-top evil was one of the reasons I was damn happy I was playing for the other side now.

Marco stood; his chest heaving, bloody weapon in his hand. The bloodied body was on the ground below him and didn't even seem to be breathing any more. I supposed the servant was dead. That's when I saw her walk by.

Eva and Louisa, escorted by a couple of armed guards, came out of the door and onto the patio, clearly on their way to the show they were putting on.

"Oh Hi ladies," Marco said to them, smiling.

Eva looked so sweet and innocent, but I saw her fight not to break into tears when she saw the dead man. She suddenly looked worried as fuck.

Marco walked toward them with the candlestick. I got up from my chair and made a beeline for her, arriving a few seconds before Marco.

"Don't you ladies look gorgeous tonight," Marco said, looking like an insane man with all the blood on his shirt. "I'm sorry you had to see this. This isn't a sight for a lady. In fact, Pablo, why the fuck are you taking them through the patio?"

The guard said nothing. He simply whisked Louisa and Eva away, into the house, and through the front door. Smart man. Better to not get into an argument with Marco, because we all knew how those ended.

"What are you all staring at? Get a fucking cleanup crew over here and clean this shit up!" Marco yelled to another servant.

A minute later, the body was carried away, and Marco was wearing a new set of white linen pants and a button down t-shirt that his servants brought out to him. He and I sat back down at the table.

"Pardon the interruption," Marco said solemnly.

"It's alright. Glad to see you are dealing with the dumb fucks in your organization appropriately," I said through gritted teeth.

Marco looked at me with a scowl, but let out a single laugh. And then another. Then he broke out into full-on raucous laughter, and I joined him.

"Yes. Good thing gazpacho is supposed to be served cold!" he said with a chuckle.

I smirked. Seeing the utter power that Marco held over his staff and the fear they had for him, I suddenly envied him. Even when I was a major drug dealer, I'd never risen to such ranks as to have people fearful of me murdering them for no reason.

"So, where were we? I believe we were discussing the terms of your agreement with us," Marco said as he took his first sip of the red gazpacho. "As I said, we want to take care of you financially for what you've done for us. In addition to the ten thousand I gave you yesterday, we have another ten here for you." He clapped, and a servant brought out another briefcase. Marco snapped it open in front of me to show me it was filled to the brim with bills.

I looked at the cash, and then glanced up at Marco. He took a sip of his wine and gauged my reaction.

"How much product I gotta move for this?"

"I'm giving you a cool thousand for every pound you move. So that's twenty pounds total."

I nodded and motioned to the man to take the cash away.

I took a long, slow sip of my wine, letting its tart, full taste linger for a moment as I did some mental math. I could make a hundred thousand cash easy if I played my cards right with Marco. I was his golden gringo, the one who knew how to sell the shit out of his product and get the most money for it.

Now, with the money in front of me, my mind started to wander. What if I took the money and fell off the face of the earth? The feds were getting me out of my sentence, but they weren't paying me shit. As soon as they got what they wanted—Luis Reyes—I'd be out on my ass on the street again, and banned from doing the only kind of business I knew: dealing coke.

"What kind of wine is this, Marco?" I said as I put the glass back down on the table.

"It's a Malbec from the high mountains in Mendoza. The only kind I drink."

"It's delicious."

Marco was starting to make a whole lot of sense. Maybe this was my chance to finally fulfill my lifelong dream of becoming a rich man who lived in the Caribbean, away from everything, with not a care in the world.

I wondered what Eva would think of my plan.

22

EVA

I woke up the next morning in a bed in the guest room mansion in a cold sweat, panicked about where I was.

I wished I was back in the regular mansion with Corbin.

It had been an interesting night, to say the least. The hundred or so members of the Reyes staff had gotten drunk, rowdy, and partied through the night as Louisa and I did a combination of bartending, stripping, and letting them take the occasional body shot. I had overheard the drunken men speaking about the whereabouts of Luis Reyes. Interestingly, many of them hadn't ever seen him. Actually, none of them had, ever.

I rolled over in the single bed I was in and sat up. Louisa slept soundly in the bed next to mine under the sheets, her chest rising and falling in the morning sun. She looked beautiful. Feminine. I wondered if Corbin had ever looked at me like I was looking at Louisa now.

Corbin. Why couldn't I get him off my mind? The sex we'd had our first night in Mexico had been under the guise of proving that I really was a prostitute. Yet when we were hooking up, it had felt more real than all the sex I'd had in my last relationship. Not fake at all.

But then there was the fact that I was fucking an ex-convict during my first field op as a DEA agent, and how wrong the logical part of my brain felt it was to do such a thing. I'm sure people in the world had done crazier things, but yeah—sleeping with your partner was a pretty big no-no. *What was I supposed to do? Report Corbin and I's relationship to HR?*

I put my feet on the ground and walked to the window, looking out over the rolling hills of the Reyes property. This was the jungle, both literally and figuratively. In isolation here, the law was not the same as the civilized world. The law here was about power, money, and sex. Marco had the power to have you killed, so he was at the top of the chain. Corbin had the power to sell Marco's cocaine, so Marco respected him. And me? My power was apparently in my sexuality, which pissed me off just a little. Marco saw me as a piece of property, and without Corbin to protect me, who knew what might become of me.

I wondered if the whole idea that I needed to even come here in the first place had been way off. Maybe I had been too bullish in requesting my promotion at just the wrong time. I glanced over at Louisa, who had seemed so relaxed yesterday putting on a show for the men, like she truly didn't have a care in the world.

I let out a loud, frustrated sigh that I couldn't have been born a man in the sixties, when sleeping with your under-cover partner was the usual *James Bond* protocol.

Louisa, stirring from my sigh, opened her eyes and caught me staring at her.

"You're up early," she said groggily. Slowly, she sat up.

"I know," I said. "I couldn't sleep once the sun came in."

She stood up and stretched her arms over her head. "Nice job last night by the way. I know you're new to this whole thing since you're just Corbin's sidepiece. You're a natural, though."

"Thanks," I replied, gathering up my things for the ride back to the main mansion. "So we should head back to the main mansion then, right?"

"Yes, but, have you ever been to the falls?"

"The falls?" I asked.

She smiled at me before getting into a sort of downward dog type pose.

"It's barely sunrise. All the men got so drunk last night, they'll be sleeping for at least another four or five hours. Let's go check out the falls. It'll be fun. I promise. We won't get in trouble."

I stiffened, but decided what the hell. I'd get to see a different side of the place. And maybe get closer to Louisa, to see if she had any information on Luis's whereabouts, since she seemed to be so entrenched in this whole operation.

"Fine. I don't have a bathing suit though."

"You won't need one," Louisa grinned.

WE HIKED a couple of miles into the backwoods of the Reyes' property in our flip flops. The cool morning air felt soothing. The sun was still very low in the sky, having not had a chance to heat up the earth yet.

"Gorgeous landscape," I said aloud to Louisa as she walked next to me.

"So you really like Corbin, don't you?" she answered, ignoring my comment.

"It's just business," I said.

"So? You're not allowed to like the guy you are doing 'business' with?" she made air quotes with her hands. "Corbin isn't like the rest of the guys who do business here. He's young and he's sexy as fuck. I saw the way you were looking at him. Don't lie."

I raised an eyebrow. I wasn't sure where she was going with this one, but Louisa was more perceptive than I had thought, so I figured I might as well bait her.

"Well, you know. Corbin is such a lady killer anyways. I'm sure he jumps from girl to girl. No sense getting attached."

Louisa's lips curved up in a soft smile, like she knew something I didn't. "Really? Why would you think that?"

I swallowed. "Well, I don't know. He just seems like the type of guy who would be with a lot of women."

"He's not like that, though."

I felt almost angry now. "How do you know that?"

Louisa stopped walking for a moment and put her leg on a fallen tree to stretch her hamstring.

"Because I tried to sleep with him a while back."

My heart raced. Corbin and my relationship was rather superficial, and we'd certainly never discussed other partners.

"And did you?"

"Yes. He said that I wasn't his type."

"Oh."

Was I Corbin's type? As much as I wanted to believe I was his special something, there was that side of me who was worried that he was a giant manwhore.

Before I could finish my response, I heard a faint rush of water.

"Come this way," she said, her speed picking up to an

almost-jog as she led the way on a faint path that zipped in and out of trees.

I followed Louisa around a rocky bend to see a 100 foot tall waterfall glistening in the sun. Under the falls were a series of rocks, and beautiful white sand lined both sides of the river where the powerful stream of water created a misty haze spreading out through parts of the stream.

Louisa turned over her shoulder and smiled at me. "Isn't it beautiful?"

It was—breathtakingly so. I smiled at the beauty of the ridiculousness of this situation. Hanging out with a prostitute in the middle of a drug lord's mansion in Mexico on an undercover mission.

Years later, I would look back on this moment and chuckle out loud, and people would wonder what I was remembering.

If I made it out of here, that is.

Louisa started to strip. I was a little shocked at first, but then why not skinny dip? After all the crazy things that had already happened on this trip, what would it matter if we took it off in the isolated jungle?

I took off my clothes, put them on a rock, and waded into the water, feeling as happy and girlish as I ever had in my life. It was so hard to believe this was work.

In that moment something pulled at my heartstrings, and I couldn't believe what it was. I wished Corbin was there with me. I dove into the water headfirst.

23

CORBIN

I went for an early run the next morning. I had a small hangover, and running had always been therapeutic for me. So I threw on some athletic shorts and gym shoes and flew out the door shirtless to take a tour of the Reyes property, waving to the armed guards on my way out.

A few minutes into my run, I noticed I had naturally started jogging toward Reyes Mansion number two, and I wasn't sure why.

Fuck that. I knew exactly why I was gravitating toward the other mansion: because *she* was there. Subconsciously, I didn't want to admit it, but I wanted to be around Eva. To check and make sure she was alright.

She's a DEA agent, she can handle herself. I kept repeating the words in my head, but I needed to know for myself that she was safe. Who knew what kind of stripper-esque things they might have made her do last night? Mobs of men could be evil.

I slapped my sweaty face. *Snap out of it.* I didn't get love-struck, and I sure as shit didn't get protective over one girl, a DEA agent no less. I had a mission--and as sexy as Eva was, I needed to focus on completing it and getting out of here alive as the first priority.

The sun began to rise higher in the sky, and I heard a waterfall in the distance, so I turned onto a dirt path that lead off the road.

A mile later, I found myself at the top of a giant waterfall. I walked out onto the edge on a rock. It was jumpable—about a hundred feet down—but it would require a skilled landing. Scanning the water beneath, I spotted something out of some kind of fairytale.

Two women—they looked like beautiful water nymphs —splashed each other in the water below, totally nude. I couldn't make out their faces through the mist, but one of them had brown hair and lighter skin, and the other had this blonde hair, coffee with cream colored skin, and what looked to be a voluptuous ass and tits. They splashed and giggled like a couple of kids in the water.

After I pinched myself to be sure that this wasn't a dream, I took a seat on a rock and just watched them for a few minutes. I was taken aback completely by how utterly joyfully they played in the water. Joy. *Eva. Eva brought joy to me.*

Fuck. Why did it always come back to her? It was only a one night stand, for God's sake! Why couldn't I just sit here and enjoy the moment, where two beautiful *naked* females were playing with each other in the wilderness. This was similar to what I had dreamt about many times over when I was locked up. Naked women. Hell, even if we had porn in prison—which we didn't—this would be ten times better. They were yelling and laughing and, one of them let out a scream that, in my dirty mind, sounded like an org—.

Holy shit. The high pitched yell was unmistakable.

Eva. She was down there.

I watched them for a couple more minutes, and then decided—fuck it—she needed a surprise.

I stood up and jumped.

When I got to the top of the water, I saw Eva and Louisa looking around for me, no doubt wondering who—or what —had just landed in the water. Their backs were turned when I poked my head out of the water, so I took a deep breath and went back under water. I opened my eyes under water and swam toward her until I ended up right behind her. As I was coming up to the surface, I extended my arm and tapped her on the shoulder.

She shrieked, and turned around to swing at me, but I stopped her arm.

"Hey," I smiled. "It's me."

Eva's eyes went wide; her chest heaved adrenaline, her erect nipples pointed right at me.

"Asshole!" she yelped and splashed me. "How dare you sneak up on me like that!"

"Wow," I said, staring at her breasts for a solid couple of seconds before moving my eyes back up to meet hers, which were sparkling, their deep brown color catching the reflection of the sun on the water. Eva opened her mouth and closed it, as if unsure of what to say to me.

"You're getting all worked up," I smiled. God she was hot when she got fired up.

Louisa, also standing in the water, stared at the awkward interaction happening between us.

"Louisa," I said, putting my hand on Eva's shoulder, "I would like to have a few moments alone with my girl, please."

Louisa shrugged and walked toward the shore where her clothes were lying.

"How the hell did you find me?" she said, seeming

stressed.

"No idea," I said honestly. *My internal Eva compass?* "But I think it's safe to say we've found another place to chat without being bugged."

"What? You don't think they've got microphones strapped to the rocks here?" she joked.

I led her by the hand over to a rock in the middle of the natural plunge pool that was half shade half sun. I hopped onto the rock and motioned for Eva to jump on top of it with me.

"I'll stay in the water, if that's fine," she said, standing in waist deep water.

"So shy all of the sudden?" I smiled, untying one of my shoes to take it off.

She didn't return my grin, her expression staying neutral. "Corbin, I've been doing some thinking. And the thing that happened two nights ago, we can't do it again. Really."

"Do you mean the thing where we only have sex? It's a little late for that."

She broke into a slight grin. "No Corbin, I mean it. I know we are acting for the cameras and all that, but I just can't do it. It's a total breach of DEA conduct, and I'm so gonna get my ass handed to me by headquarters if they find out that you and I were together."

I stared back at her gorgeous brown eyes, letting go of my smile for a moment. "So you didn't enjoy what we did the other night. It *was* just an act."

"That's not important. What's important is that we adhere to policy."

I tilted my head, taking off my other shoe. "Right. Policy." *What was really bothering her?* "I don't get you, Eva."

"You and me," she said, pointing at both of us in succession, "Cannot be a thing. I'm afraid I've made a big mistake."

"You made a big mistake...*twice.*"

She rolled her eyes. "Yes."

"I don't get you Eva, what is your deal?"

She folded her arms, naked, which made her little 'this is a taboo romance' tirade even sexier to me.

"My deal, Corbin, is I should never have slept with you. If you had told me who you were up front, I wouldn't have done it. But you lied by omission. You played a dirty trick. And now..."

She trailed off and looked at the falls; the early morning sun was creeping over some trees and casting a light on her body from the neck up.

"That's not it," I said, leaning forward and nudging her chin with the back of my curved finger. "There's something else. Tell me."

Eva stayed silent. Eva definitely had her guard up in a weird way. She'd let me ravage her in bed, but she hadn't let me all the way in by any means. Emotionally, she was hiding something from me.

"What are you thinking about right now?" I asked.

"I don't want to talk about it," she answered, turning away from me.

My gym shoes off and drying in the sun, I slid into the water and stood next to her.

"I feel...guilty about my last relationship," she said.

"Guilty. Okay." I looked at her eyes and saw her twisting in pain. Clearly I was pushing her out of her comfort zone.

"I feel guilty because," she took a deep breath, "I cheated on Ned. That's why our relationship ended."

Bombshell. Two of them. "You dated *Ned?* Like, DEA Ned? Doesn't seem like your type at all."

"Yes! And DEA Ned was actually a nice guy. But I ruined

everything because of one drunken mistake. And now, I'm here with you *playing* being a mistress. But in reality, it's true. I *am* just a mistress type of girl." She frowned.

I didn't say anything. I looked down at her and then I extended my palm around her neck and massaged her.

"You've never cheated on anyone, have you?" she asked.

I actually laughed out loud, which I guess wasn't the most sensitive response, because she swiped my arm away from her body.

"Dick," she mouthed under her breath and turned away from me.

"Hey, I didn't mean it like that." I stiffened, and considered how to answer her question.

She half-turned toward me, her arms crossed. "Well then how did you mean it, other than to say that my question was stupid?"

"Your question isn't that stupid. I've never cheated on anyone. Well, now that I think about it, I've never been in a real relationship that's lasted more than a couple of months."

I massaged my temple with my thumb and forefinger. Eva was leading me to a revelation of my own.

"Huh, what?"

"It's stupid. You'll laugh."

She opened up her body language and took a step toward me. "Tell me. I promise I won't judge."

"No, forget it. It's not something guys talk about."

She wrapped her hand around my bicep and looked up at me. "I'm standing here baring my soul to you—literally, I'm naked—and you can't tell me what comes to your mind? Wow. I am just an expert when it comes to finding emotionally closed-off guys."

Her gaze didn't leave my face. She just kept staring innocently up at me with those beautiful dark eyes, requesting that I share my darkest secrets with her. I looked off into the distance for a moment, my eyes following the sightline of the river, which seemed to go on forever.

"Fine. I had a girlfriend toward the end of freshman year of high school. One of those ridiculous, make-out by the locker room kind of romances. Never cheated on her."

"Why are you talking about your high-school sweetheart right now?"

I smirked. "I thought you said you wouldn't judge what I was thinking about."

"Touché."

I continued. "So my mom did a lot of drugs—crack, meth, pot—you name it. It was a lot for a teenager to handle. And one day early sophomore year, I came home and my mom was gone. She left a note that said she wasn't a good mother with the number for child services for us to get in touch with. I never saw her again, and eventually found out she passed away. And as far as girls go, I didn't really have time for a girlfriend since I was providing for our family, albeit through the illicit means of dealing drugs."

Eva was an arm's length away and she took another step toward me, eclipsing the remaining distance so that her skin was almost touching me.

"Holy shit," she said, her eyes glazed over. I thought I saw a tear stream down one cheek, but I wasn't sure if it was just mist from the waterfall. She moved her body closer to mine and wrapped me in a hug. I was a little surprised that she was hugging me naked after the whole 'not going to sleep with you anymore' tangent that she had just gone on, but her soft body felt amazing against mine, and I loved the way she nuzzled her head into my chest, almost like a golden retriever.

We hugged for a good long minute. She sniffled, answering my question as to whether or not the drop was from the water or a tear.

I realized that what I had just told Eva, I had never told a soul. Not my brother Casey, not my counselor in prison, not any of my friends. And it felt fucking good to let it out.

We released each other. Eva ran her hand through my hair.

"Hey," she said. "It's not your fault. None of this. Not your mom being a coward and leaving you, not the fact that you got wrapped up in drugs, nothing."

"Thanks," I shot back. "It's not your fault either."

She scrunched her face in a quizzical look. "What do you mean?"

"You act like I'm the only one here who is in confessional mode right now. You blame yourself for cheating on Ned. I'm not a betting man any more, but I would bet the relationship was on the way out when that happened. And that, Eva, isn't your fault. Stop blaming yourself."

She paused and thought for a moment, her hands on her hips. Then she opened her mouth like a lightbulb had just gone off in her head.

"Oh. My. Gosh. You're right. Ned had ignored me for weeks when I did it. I was at the point of stalking him on a Friday night when he said we couldn't hang out."

We let our respective revelations hang in the air for a few moments. I didn't know what else to say, so I just slipped my hands down to her sides, grabbed her, and kissed the shit out of her.

Her body fit against mine like a puzzle piece, her every curve molding into my muscles.

I was the one with the guilty conscience now, considering my getaway plan.

24

CORBIN

Later that evening, Marco, Eva, Louisa and I sat on the patio back at the big mansion sharing a bottle of wine, our chairs in a circle as we watched the sun go down. I felt like we were no closer to finding Luis Reyes than when we were back in San Diego. Personally, I was getting more and more curious as to his whereabouts. He was the leader of the biggest cocaine cartel in the world and this was his hideaway. Where else would he be? Something smelled funny, and I intended to find out what.

Plus, Marco kept droning on about how badly he wanted to spend a night with Alexa, which was starting to get to me. No way was I letting her alone with that psychopath, much less after what he did to his innocent employee last night.

"Alexa, I'd really like for you to spend a night with me. Trust me. I will make it worth your while," Marco sneered.

I wanted to jump across the table and slap Marco. *Just let it go, man.* I decided a good natured ribbing would be a better route.

"You really want to get my sloppy seconds," I jabbed.

Marco leaned in toward me, his elbows on the table. "I'm

fine with you warming her up for me," he said. "I don't care if I'm first or fiftieth, I just want her. With me. Alone."

I held on to my stone face even as I threw up a little bit in my mouth. She was mine and only mine, and Marco wasn't getting anywhere near her. No way in hell was I allowing this to go on.

"Corbin? Did you hear what I said?"

Shit. I'd spaced the hell out into my own little world again.

"Sorry," I said. "I was calculating all of the money I am going to make when I pull this deal off."

"Ha. You *would* be thinking about money. Money and women, those are Corbin Young's priorities," he grinned.

"Obviously," Eva said without looking at me.

Louisa sat there twirling her hair, drinking her wine and looking off into the horizon, either purposely ignoring us, or just generally oblivious to our conversation. Either way, I envied her. It must have been nice to be so worry free.

"I deal with a lot of assholes in my line of work," Eva said, stealing a glance at me. "So it's nothing new."

Marco finished the rest of his wine and slammed his glass down on the wooden table. He reached across the table and grabbed Eva's wrist. "I'm a little concerned that Corbin is spending too much time with you, though. We have so many women here—I can have one ordered for you, Corbin. I worry that you aren't accepting my hospitality."

Or are you worried that since I'm spending all of my time with Alexa, you haven't had the opportunity to have your way with her?

My possessive streak bubbled over. I didn't give a shit if he was the boss or not, I needed to draw a line in the sand. "Dammit Marco! I'm not too concerned that I'm giving my woman a good nightly fuck. The way she services me, there's just not a real reason for me to get someone new right now. No offense Louisa, I'm sure you're great."

"None taken," Louisa shrugged. She ran her tongue lightly around her lips and took another sip of her wine.

"I am, however, concerned that we have been here for two days, and Luis Reyes still hasn't made an appearance. Marco, where is he?"

"I will take you to him," Marco said. "But first, I want a night with Alexa," he smiled.

I felt my insides tighten.

"That wasn't the goddamn deal we set up. At no point did we talk about that."

"The offer has changed," Marco said, cocking his head to one side.

"You know what? I'm doing you a favor. You *need* me to sell to college kids. You enlisted me for this job! And now you're making demands. That is not how this works."

Marco leaned back in his chair and folded his hands. The moonlight was starting to replace the sunlight, and he looked extra menacing.

"You are my friend, yes, Corbin. But right now you do not make the demands. I make the demands." He moved his eyes to the several armed thugs surrounding our table.

"You are my friend, too, Marco. Which is why I'm going to let this go. Must be the wine." I scooted out my chair and stood up. "Alexa. Come."

She looked at Marco, then at me, like a dog between two masters. Marco said nothing.

"Thank you for dinner," Eva said politely.

Two of the thugs stopped us as we made our way to the door. "Jefe, what should we do with them? That's some major disrespect, no?"

Marco got out of his chair and slowly approached us. He had the rubik's cube in his hand now, tossing it up and playing with it. It was totally solved except for the corners. He put his face six inches from mine, scowled and cocked his head.

I wondered if he might just kill us both, right then. Shit, he was certainly crazy enough.

"Tonight," Marco began, "I'm going to let this go. But tomorrow we will have a serious business discussion. I think the wine has started to affect your head."

25

EVA

Corbin escorted me up the stairs. Once we were inside our room, I slammed the door behind us, managing to maintain a semblance of control in front of the video camera. "Corbin. I think we need to jump in the *shower.*"

If he was half as good with women as Marco claimed Corbin was, he'd understand the added verbiage that my eyes put in the phrase.

Right. Fucking. Now.

A million thoughts flashed through my mind as I tore off my dress and my jewelry. How I should have listened to Ned. How this whole mission was a mistake. How we almost just died. How we were so fucked now, like royally-fucked-we-are-going-to-get-killed fucked because Corbin couldn't stop running his mouth.

I turned the shower on full power, and the water was piping hot. I didn't care and jumped in. Corbin stepped in right behind me.

"Jesus! Ouch! Are you crazy?" Corbin jumped at the heat

of the shower. It was legitimately scalding, so I wasn't surprised that he recoiled.

"Am I crazy? Screw you. You are the one who is legitimately insane."

"Oh yea? I'm insane. Please, enlighten me how."

Corbin adjusted the water temperature so it was still hot, but now it was tolerable. He ducked his head under the water and wet his hair.

"Well, let's see. Number one you just told Marco to fuck off."

"More or less. Your point?"

"So there is no way he's going to lead us to Luis now."

"That's where you're wrong. But go ahead with whatever you have to say."

Dick.

"Moving on to number two. He's going to kill us. He's just biding his time. I know it," I said.

Corbin grabbed a bar of soap and started to lather himself up. "Nah. We're good. Trust me."

My blood boiled at the cocky bastard's attitude.

"I thought you were a little dense, but clearly you are just dumb. I think all of those drugs have slowed down your brain. Don't you see what you've *done?*"

I grabbed the soap from him. Even my lather was aggressive. I looked up and noticed Corbin was smirking at me.

"What the hell are you looking at?"

"You. You're extra sexy when you're angry."

My jaw dropped. Unbelievable. Corbin Young was an asshole, I trusted him completely, and now I was going to lose my life because of that choice.

And you know what else was unbelievable? The cocky bastard was turning me on.

"You're unbelievable. We're done. Whatever we had a

couple of nights—that's over. It was unprofessional, and I can't believe I did it. And the worst part is, it's affecting you!"

"Yes, it is affecting me."

I glanced below Corbin's waist, and he was starting to enlarge. *Fuck that's hot.* But no more. I fought the feeling welling up inside me. *Not a good idea.*

A light bulb went off in my head.

"You don't want me to spend time with Marco alone. You're jealous. Which is stupid."

Corbin chuckled. "Jealous? Oh, are we dating now? I must have missed the memo."

"Get serious, Corbin! You are getting possessive of me. And it's making Marco suspicious! I'm supposed to be your fucking mistress, your property to be shared. Not your girl-friend! You're not supposed to guard me; you're supposed to just pass me around."

Corbin took a deep breath. He placed his hand on my neck and started massaging it, just like he had under the waterfall earlier. I was angry, but his fingers felt so damn good I let him leave his hand there.

"Possessiveness has *nothing* to do with how I acted back there. It's about respect. Do you know what people like Marco respect? They respect it when you have a spine and you stick up for yourself. So I told him to go fuck himself. Called his bluff. This is all one giant poker game."

I crossed my arms, unconvinced. "So you're saying you aren't possessive of me at all."

Corbin swallowed and his chest muscles flexed. "Yeah I like you. I do. But my motivations for my actions here are purely based on me getting the DEA what they need to let me off my sentence. How I feel about you—" he intensified the neck massage, "has nothing to do with how I act with Marco. Business is business."

"Your hand feels good," I said, almost reflexively. Amazing, actually. Suddenly, I remembered that we were both naked in the shower. Corbin was staring back at me with his intense blues. His Adam's apple moved again.

"What are you thinking about right now?" he asked me.

"That's my move," I said. "What are *you* thinking about?"

"You."

My heart felt like it dropped out of my chest cavity. I stepped back and felt my back press up against the cold tile. I let out a noise halfway between a moan and a sigh.

"I feel something special for you," Corbin said. "Tell me you feel something too."

"I feel something too," I whispered. Corbin pressed his muscular chest against my soft breasts. His sharp jaw lingered inches from my face.

"I admit it," he growled. "I don't want to see you with Marco. I want you all to myself."

I ran my hand down his wet, soapy chest, and he returned the favor.

"Me too," I moaned.

26

CORBIN

My mouth smashed Eva's, and she was mine again. Her lips felt like soft pillows, a haven for body and my soul. I pressed her soft body up against the hard tile wall, our bodies slick with soap and suds. She rubbed the back of my head with her hand ever so gently, and worked her way down my back, my hip, until she wrapped her delicate fingers around my cock.

I let out a low, throaty growl. She looked up at me with her baby brown eyes. I had never wanted anyone more in my life.

I wanted her so bad that the L-word ran through my mind, involuntarily.

Love. Where the fuck did that thought come from?

The L-word had never come close to crossing my mind before, but here I was in this strange, life-or-death situation with a girl I'd only known for three days and I'd never been so sure of anything in my life.

I love Eva.

The thought brought an intensity to our kissing that I'd never felt before. On a one to ten scale, we were at eleven.

My lips opened, and I couldn't say the L-word, but at least something came out. "I've never wanted anyone more in my life."

"Shut up and keep kissing me," she said.

Fuck I want her.

I devoured her mouth with mine. One arm hooked around her and the other pressed into the wall to hold our balance. I wanted to feel every ounce of her skin against my own.

I pushed her to the back wall of the shower and got down on my knees to taste her. She lifted one leg up and I dove between her legs with my tongue.

"Oh my God. Oh my God. Oh my..." she gyrated her hips in motion with my mouth. She lightly massaged a tussle of my hair as I pleasured her. Fuck me if I'd ever been so turned on in my life by the soft moans coming from her mouth.

I put a finger on her clit, rubbing gently in circles. Her moaning intensified.

"Ungh. Corbin. Unghhh..."

She convulsed and hummed, her sweet submissive moan turning me hard as a rock. As if she could read my mind, she pushed my forehead out from in between her legs.

"Corbin, I need you inside me. *Now.*"

"Yes," I growled, needing her just as much.

I stood up and turned her body around. She put her hands on the wall and looked over her shoulder at me, brushing her blond hair behind her ear. I took a moment and just admired her beautiful being from behind. Her beautiful, round ass was pointed straight at me and her tits dangled. Her long hair was wet, and her make-up had washed off, revealing her beautiful true skin to me.

She'd never looked hotter.

"Please," she said.

I smiled. The sexiest woman I had ever met was wet as hell in front of me, begging me to fuck her.

I leaned forward and kissed her on the neck. "Eva, baby. You're so beautiful. You're fucking incredible."

She closed her eyes and kissed me. She reached her arm back between her legs, found my thick hardness, and guided me inside her.

She hummed softly as I entered her.

She felt fucking *incredible.*

I wanted to do this with her every day for the rest of my life.

We started slow and sensual as she got used to me filling her up.

I leaned down, took her breasts in my hands and kissed her again. I wanted every inch of her body, mind and soul.

A few minutes later she got every inch of me, and the wet *slap slap slap* sound was heard over Eva's moans.

She is heaven.

Soon I found *the spot* again and we hit our rhythm together. She interspersed "Oh God's" with "yes's" and "Corbin's," and we were taken to that higher place.

I wanted to scream her name, but I couldn't. *Eva.*

"Oh God, Alexa," I grunted.

She looked over her shoulder at me. "Say it again, baby," she purred.

"Alexa, you are so fucking sexy," I growled.

Her hair bounced up and down along with the rest of her body.

"I'm coming, baby." She grinded her body against mine and my hips smashed her in perfect rhythm. "Right there..."

She let out one more light moan and I lost it and became

a wild caveman. I was bucking her as hard as I could against the wall. I loved feeling my hips right up against her flesh.

"Eva, baby, I'm going to come," I managed to say. "Where do you want me to come?"

"Come on my tits." We pulled away from each other for a painful second. She kneeled in front of me and grabbed hold of my slick cock.

She aimed me right at her breasts, and I deposited an impressive amount of come on them. That's what happened when you fucked the hottest girl you'd ever met, I supposed.

She looked up at me with puppy dog eyes and I wished I'd had a phone to take a photo of the sexiest pose I'd ever seen.

This was the moment I knew I was totally fucked.

I was in love with Eva Napleton, and there were some very big reasons that this was a problem.

I gently touched her face and guided her back up. *Should I tell her how I feel?*

"Eva, I..."

I was losing my mind. I really did want to do this with her every day for the rest of my life.

"You what?" she asked. God, she was so fucking vulnerable. I needed to tell her. We could die tonight for God's sake.

"I think we should wash up," I smiled. I kissed her.

We stepped back into the shower and soaped up again.

"Corbin, I..." she stammered, searching for words just like I did. "I think that was the single hottest experience of my life."

"You want to go again?" I raised an eyebrow.

Her eyes started at my face and worked their way down my chest and abs before landing around my thighs.

I'll take that as a yes.

27

EVA

Despite my freak out, Marco didn't kill us that night. Or the next night, or the next. Although I hated to admit it, Corbin was right about Marco. After Corbin stood up to Marco that night, Marco stopped messing with us so much. Which basically turned our stay into a sort of a vacation, with the way Corbin and I had been...getting along.

It had been almost two weeks since we first arrived. According to Marco, Luis had been on a trip to the Caribbean, but he would be getting here 'soon.'

We were both starting to get a little antsy that we still hadn't found Luis. Back at base, they were probably freaking out.

And here Corbin and I were just enjoying ourselves.

The sunlight streamed into our room and I opened my eyes. Corbin was naked, sleeping spread eagle on the bed. Good thing it was a king size because the man took up a lot of room. I inched toward him and hovered my face over his, taking in his scent. I lightly ran my hand from his shoulder on down his chest and abs, not wanting to wake him.

After our conversation under the waterfall, our relationship had spurred beyond solely a physical thing. I felt comfortable around Corbin mentally, too. I let my guard down. I had made more love with him in two weeks than I had with Ned in the entire last year of our relationship. I didn't know if that said more about how shitty me and Ned's relationship was, or how electric Corbin and I's connection was—probably both. Not to mention I hadn't faked a single orgasm with Corbin.

Damn, I was getting horny just running my hand on his muscles. I ran my hand over his leg and I swore I saw his cock twitch a bit. He took a deep breath and I could tell he was still sleeping.

Corbin and I had gotten really comfortable with each other through the last couple of weeks. We'd even started a running joke that we'd make in front of Marco. I would say very sexual, submissive things, conveying that the only reason I was there was to please Corbin sexually. This might have offended my sensibilities in a previous life. But knowing that Corbin was so completely and utterly concerned with *my* pleasure made me more than fine with it. I loved having an inside joke between us.

I slid my hand down the V of his abs. I couldn't help myself and I wrapped my fingers around his cock. Not even in a sexual way...just in an *I'm curious* kind of way. Could guys get hard in their sleep?

I looked into the camera and smiled. I wondered if Marco was watching us this early in the morning. *Maybe I should give him a little show, just in case.*

Since when did I think like this?

Corbin had rubbed off on me, the little sexual deviant. I meant that in the best way possible. He brought out the

Alexa in me. In fact, I was starting to enjoy living the life of this very sexual alter ego.

The crazy thing was that I was *falling* for him. The whole crazy "pretend I'm his personal prostitute" thing had made me feel closer to him than any man I had ever been with. I felt like I had the license to be naughty in bed and he wouldn't judge me, no matter what.

And somehow...that made our connection deeper? But that made no sense. *Logic, Eva, use logic.*

You're a DEA agent, he's a criminal. After you catch Luis Reyes, you two are done.

Sure, he was damaged, but weren't we all in some way? I knew Corbin had a rap sheet a mile long, but everybody deserves a second chance, right?

I stroked his length, up and down. I hadn't gone down on a guy in so long. But if anyone deserves a morning wake up, it was Corbin. He hadn't even asked one time for me to go down on him. With Ned, it was him begging me every night and it seemed like such a chore.

Corbin groaned, stirring. I was nervous, but I crawled over and got directly on his side, perpendicular to his body for easy access. I tied my hair in a ponytail behind my head, and put my hand back on his cock. Slowly, I leaned my head down, opened my mouth and licked his shaft on the sides.

He opened his eyes and they darted immediately toward mine.

"Eva," he growled, his voice gravelly. My heart beat harder, and I didn't know if it was because he used my real name, or if it was because I felt like I might have surprised him with something I wasn't sure if he'd like. Maybe he'd be freaked out by my morning enthusiasm.

"Yes?" I answered, grinning.

"You have never looked more sexy than you do right now, in the morning sun."

I didn't know why his words cut right through me, but they did. They made me shudder and sent goose bumps all over my skin. I felt so naughty for rising early to go down on him for no particular reason. Yet his words were soft, the vibrations of his voice so low.

I smiled and returned to what I started, slowing licking his length up and down a few more times. I lingered on his tip before taking him in my mouth.

He moaned louder and reached out to massage my head. He gyrated his hips in motion with my head until we found a rhythm. My eyes closed, I put one hand out and touched his abs, feeling his hardness with my tongue.

"Honey, open your eyes," he said, touching my chin. "I want to see you."

I looked up to see Corbin staring back at me, and a muffled *mmmmm* sound came out of my mouth. His hands dropped from my head to my back, and I became more enthusiastic with every bob of my head.

"Stop," he said, softly but sternly.

I removed my head from his cock.

"Why?" I murmured.

"I want you to ride me, baby."

Just the thought of him sliding inside me made me wet.

"I thought you'd never ask," I smiled.

I straddled him and slowly guided his cock into me, one inch at a time.

"You're already wet," he smirked, a little shocked.

"Is it weird that going down on you got me warmed up?"

He was about to respond, but his eyes rolled up in the back of his head as I swallowed him up with my body, and all that came out was a gurgled "Fuck yeah."

I started out slowly, grinding up and down on his length. Then faster. Then heaven. And I became an animal again.

I always thought sex with Corbin couldn't get any better. And then something like this would happen. I grinded on him, and he played my hips in perfect motion, like I was the ying to his yang.

This was what happened when you had motion in the ocean *and* a nice big boat.

I LOST track of the time, but when I came to, Corbin and I were cuddling and the sun was a lot higher in the sky than it was when we started. His big arms were wrapped around me and I nestled into him, the back of my body feeling every square inch of his muscles I was able to.

"Hey," he whispered.

"Hey yourself."

"I need to tell you something."

"So say it."

"I know this is crazy. Really crazy, but I have to tell you."

"Corbin. What the hell is it?" I recoiled back to examine his face. For once, he didn't have that typical shit eating grin on his face.

"I'm in love with you," he said, and watched my face as the words sank in.

Adrenaline surged through my heart. I swallowed hard. My mind went a thousand different places. This was so fast for the L-word. *How good is the audio on that goddamn camera Marco setup?*

As crazy as it was, I felt the same way. Then there were five bangs on the door that would be too loud to be called just a 'knock.'

"Corbin. It's Marco. I need you now. We need to talk. Bring that whore of yours with you. We'll meet on the patio in five."

"Okay," Corbin barked back.

We looked each other in the eye.

"I guess we better go," Corbin said, moving to put his clothes on. "We can finish this conversation later."

28

CORBIN

Eva and I quickly dressed and walked down the stairs, led by two armed guards. They took us outside and pointed us in the direction of the shaded patio table, which had a spread of fruit, coffee, and assorted breads and vegetables.

A pit formed in my stomach for two reasons. One, I had just confessed to Eva my love for her, and she hesitated. Despite the untimely interruption, when I looked in her eyes I had no idea if she loved me back. Many girls in the past had told me the same and I'd looked at them like a deer in the headlights, only to take a slap to the face from the girl after.

Now, Eva had given me a little taste of my own medicine. Unreturned love had the ability to make a person feel like shit. As I felt right now.

But secondly, and perhaps more life threatening at the moment, I had a very bad feeling about the way Marco had come up to get us. In the past two whole weeks he had never been so expedient about meeting with us. And he never personally came to invite us places, either.

"Corbin. Alexa," Marco said, standing up and nodding toward us both as we neared the table. "Thank you for joining me. I didn't know how long you were planning on staying cooped up in that little guest room of ours, so I decided I would take it upon myself to get you two down here. Please, sit."

The servants pulled out our chairs, and we sat.

"Quite the show you put on this morning," Marco said. The maid filled Eva and I's cups full of coffee. I added in some fresh cream.

"The fuck are you talking about?" I belted back. Was he just going to openly talk about how he was just jacking off to a video of Eva and I this morning? *Have a little respect.*

"Stop being modest," Marco retorted. "I'm pretty sure the entire second floor could hear you two."

"Were we really that loud? Shit. My bad." I smirked. Although Eva was the one making most of the noise, to be fair.

"Right. Actually, that's why I wanted to talk to you this morning. First of all, Luis Reyes will be in later this afternoon. We'll talk, he'll give you your shipment of pure cocaine, and you'll be on your merry way to sell it to the college students. How does that sound?"

"Sounds like a fucking plan. I love Mexico, Marco, but to be honest I'm starting to get a little antsy, you know?"

"Of course you are. Second, I wanted to apologize."

"Apologize?"

"Yes, for doubting your loyalty before. All simply because you wouldn't let me spend a night with Alexa. That was childish of me."

My spider sense was going off. Marco almost never apologized to anyone unless he was trying to butter you up for something. I took a sip of my coffee and stole a nonchalant glance at Eva. She had the same sexy smile on her face but her nervousness was palpable to me. Hopefully Marco didn't recognize it.

"Hey, listen Marco, we can let bygones be bygones. I meet Luis later today, shake hands and all that, get the product, and bam—" I slapped my hands together, "I'm on my way to San Diego to get those college kids lit with snow. I take half, and everyone's happy."

"Oh yes. Half will be just fine."

I was a little shocked that Marco wasn't trying to run a harder bargain.

"On one condition," he continued.

"Ah, there it is." I leaned back in my chair. "Hit me."

"I am going to trade mistresses for a day with you. Louisa came back from her trip from San Diego today, and you can be with her while I take Alexa. No more negotiating on this point. Let's call it a last day celebration."

I laughed. God Dammit he was driving a hard bargain. I *had* been overly protective of her. I looked over at Eva and put my hand on her knee. She barely had any makeup on and she was hotter than anyone I'd seen at this frickin place. I think she knew it, too. Marco knew it. Hell, the entire staff could see the self-evident truth.

"I just don't know, Marco. Maybe you're right that I want her all to myself. Maybe I'm a selfish bastard."

Marco rocked back in his chair, folded his hands, and nodded. "I also had a feeling you'd say that. But I'm not giving you another option, Corbin. I want Alexa. She's just hired help for you, right? So what's the big deal? You *do want this deal,* don't you Corbin?"

I gulped. *Fuck this guy.* If I said no, he'd think I'm not earnest. If I said yes, he'd take Eva and do...God knew what with her. My eyes darted to Eva, who had been silent during the whole exchange.

"It's going to cost you extra," she finally said, and squeezed my knee under the table, perhaps trying to comfort me.

My heart dropped. Was she really voluntarily going with him?

"Don't worry, honey," Marco said. He nodded and had one of his flunkies bring a briefcase over filled with cash. They opened it in front of Eva.

"That enough for you?"

Eva smiled softly like tens of thousands of dollars weren't a big deal to her. "That'll work."

She was in full-on Alexa mode. Playing her role like she had to. But I didn't want her to be Alexa anymore. I wanted Eva back, and I wanted her all to myself.

But there was nothing I could do right now.

"Very well then. It's time for your...shall we say, extended personal tour. Come this way." Marco got up and reached his arm out to Eva.

I swallowed. *This isn't happening.*

"Enjoy your afternoon with Louisa," he said, and looked at his watch. "Luis will be here around three. That gives us a solid three hours for *siestas* with our women."

I raced through my mind in an attempt to find some kind of last ditch plan to save Eva from Marco, but they quickly disappeared into the mansion. Armed guards closed the door behind him and shot me a menacing look.

Louisa walked up to me and put her hand on my shoulder.

"Well Corbin. I suppose we are going to get to hang out after all, aren't we?!"

She was beautiful, bubbly, and cheery. But she wasn't

Eva, and I couldn't hang out with her sober while every second I kept thinking about what Marco and Eva were doing together all alone. I motioned for the maid to come over.

"Can you please bring me something to drink?"

"It's not even noon sir."

"I know what time it is. Bring me a tequila on the rocks."

"Yes sir."

"Oh, morning drinking! Yay!" Louisa said, and sat on my lap.

It was funny how now that I knew Eva—the complete package— a beautiful woman like Louisa could suddenly seem like an annoying ditz who I wanted nothing to do with in comparison.

The maid brought out two glasses of tequila. I reluctantly clinked glasses with Louisa.

"Ching ching!" She said. She wasn't a bad person, really. I decided maybe I should give her a chance and tried to face the facts.

In spite of how hot our sex had been, maybe Eva never loved me to begin with.

And maybe I had better just start accepting that fact, and move on to the part where I took the money and ran.

29

EVA

I walked with Marco to a separate wing of the mansion. He had his hand on the small of my back and it was creeping me the fuck out.

I couldn't believe what I had just done. As soon as the words came out of my mouth, I regretted them. *Sure, I'll sleep with you. How much money do you have?*

How is it that those words came out of my mouth instinctually just so I could convincingly play the role of Alexa, but when I was *actually* in love with a man I couldn't tell him.

"I'm so happy to have you for the afternoon," he said. "Corbin has always been quite protective of his women. All of them."

He said it as though Corbin had been chasing tail for years. "All of his women?"

"Yes, he's had many. You didn't think you were the only one, did you?" he laughed.

Maybe not the only one, but a very special one.

"Of course not."

Marco opened a door, let me in, and flicked the lights on

illuminating a large room. The space inside looked surprisingly modern in comparison with the rest of the old fashioned mansion. Dual monitors sat on a large wooden desk with a keyboard and mouse on top. Behind the desk was a king sized bed.

"Welcome to the control room. AKA my bedroom." Marco pursed his lips and angled his mustache up on the sides. I resisted cringing as I took a seat on his bed.

"Wow," I said, trying to sound ditzy. "You've got a real big fancy computer."

"Do you like computers?" He walked over and sat down at his desk.

"Well I don't use them much—my family is very poor, you know—but yes, I'm interested in them. I've never seen two computers next to each other like that."

What the hell am I even saying? "I'm interested in computers?" Was that a real statement? I'd say anything to delay Marco from sitting next to me on the bed.

"Well let me show you what I do with this little thing. Come over here," he said.

He moved the mouse and the home screen came on. He clicked on an icon and a program loaded.

"Why don't you have a seat, *mi amor*," he reiterated when I didn't move, and patted his thigh.

I gulped and had a weird *déjà vu* moment, picturing the first time I met Marco in the bar. I wanted to slap him across the face and tell him that wasn't his *love*. But I couldn't. So I strutted over to him and sat down on his lap with a generic smile on my face.

"Corbin does know how to pick a good woman. You are beautiful, Alexa. I have a confession to make."

"A confession? Don't worry, I'll forgive you," I giggled—

hopefully not too fakely—and tapped his nose with my index finger in a flirty sort of way.

"Oh, *mi amor*, you are too kind. Let me show you, here."

He pointed to the screen. He had pulled up a camera feed to Corbin and I's room.

"I've been watching you and Corbin when you...do your thing."

My heart dropped. But not because my suspicions about Marco watching us were confirmed—the creep. The sick fuck.

On the contrary, my heart dropped because of what I saw on the screen: Corbin sitting next to Louisa in our room on the bed. Her arm was on his bicep and it looked like they were sharing a tender moment.

For a millisecond, I wished I could jump into the screen and attack her like in some crazy sci-fi movie. What right did she have...?

And what is Corbin thinking?

"Does this thing have audio? It actually kind of turns me on to listen to other people," I said. I needed to hear what they were saying. I wanted to know how much of our pillow talk Marco had been able to hear. Sometimes, Corbin and I would whisper things to each other that we maybe shouldn't have in case Marco was listening, but we'd do it softly.

"Really?! I must admit I'm a little surprised you like that kind of thing. Of course it has audio. I'll turn it on."

Marco clicked a button and their voices were instantly as clear as an HD movie.

Shit. That is some clear damn audio.

"Where are the microphones for this?"

"Little microchips fit really nicely in the middle of the pillow," Marco said. He turned the volume up on the audio so we could hear them both speaking loud and clear.

My heart sank.

What else had Marco heard? Corbin confessing his love for me? Something suddenly seemed very *off*.

Louisa spoke first. "I mean I always found you very attractive, Corbin."

"Let's just do what we came here to do," Corbin said.

My eyes bulged out of my head. Was he really going to hook up with her?

"Why so serious?" Louisa answered, and then she grabbed Corbin's face and plopped a big kiss on his lips. Corbin didn't fight it off.

"Turn it off," I said. I held back tears, trying to keep the smile on my face, but one escaped and rolled down my cheek. Marco clicked out of it and the audio turned off.

I tried to wipe the tear but Marco grabbed my arm before I could.

"Oh, are you sad, *mi amor?*" Marco cocked his head and pursed his lips. He reached a finger out and wiped the tear for me.

"No, I'm not," I scrunched my face. "Why would I be?"

Marco patted my back a couple of times and I stood up, getting out of his lap. He stood up, walked over to his desk and opened up a drawer. He turned toward me with a scowl on his face and a gun in his hand.

"Oh, I don't know *Eva*. Why don't you tell me?"

My heart beat out of its chest, like I had just started heading down a rollercoaster. I felt physically dizzy, like I'd just been hit with a ton of adrenaline bricks.

"Eva? What do you mean, *papi?*" I acted confused and stared seductively into Marco's eyes as he walked toward me.

"Oh *mi amor*, please don't take me for a fool," he said. He snapped his fingers and two men came in from outside and grabbed me by either arm. Marco leaned in and whispered in my ear. "You've done that enough already. And fools die much faster. So let's stop playing games."

I stared at him, but I had nothing to say. Then I gasped, remembering what Corbin had said to me earlier this morning. He'd used my real name many times over in bed—even though he'd only whispered it.

"Put her in the chair and tie her up," Marco said to a couple of security guards. "We've got a double agent on our hands."

30

CORBIN

E va was gone and she didn't even love me in the first place, *so fuck it.*

I was pretty much done in Mexico. I would take the money and the coke, sell it on the down-low in San Diego, and then get the fuck out of the drug trade and away from the DEA's grasp before they knew I was gone.

Hey, if they couldn't catch Luis Reyes in over two years of searching for him, I was sure I could stay ahead of them if I hid somewhere south of the border.

Louisa and I walked up the stairs to my room. I held her by the hand as I led her, but any kind of hook up was the last thing on my mind. I just wanted to get a little information out of her. Because this Luis Reyes shit, after two weeks of being there, was driving me up a wall. *Where was the guy?* Was he a ghost? I didn't even care if the DEA found their information, but I had to know for *me.*

We took a seat on my bed.

"Louisa, I need you to be totally honest with me. Okay? Let's just sit down on the bed for a second."

"I mean I always found you very attractive, Corbin." Not

what I meant at *all*, but I didn't want to piss her off since I was trying to get information from her.

"Let's just do what we came here to do," I said.

"Why so serious?" she leaned over and gave me a big kiss right on the lips.

I was pissed but surprised, and it took me a second to push her off. "What are you doing?"

"What I came here to do," she smiled. "You. Just like Marco told me to."

I stood up and paced around the room for a moment, needing to put distance between the two of us. "Listen, I need to know what Marco has been saying about me, about Luis, anyone. Anything at all. Talk to me."

She shrugged and flopped her hands backward on the bed. "Oh, I don't know. I mean last night when I got in from San Diego, he mumbled something about having solved that rubik's cube last night while we were having sex. Sort of weird dirty talk."

I froze in my tracks and swallowed hard. "He talked about the rubik's cube...*while you were having sex?*"

Louisa shrugged, seeming pretty unphased. "Yeah. I mean he always yells out weird shit during sex, and he likes pillow talk too. I dunno. Let's see. Anything weird..."

"Come here." I took her by the hand, led her to the bathroom, and turned on the shower as high as the pressure would go. I didn't disrobe and we didn't get in. I just prayed the water was loud enough while we kept our clothes on. If Marco had found the chip, I was fucked. And not in the way that I liked Eva to fuck me. Like, royally, Marco-would-bust-out-a-gun-and-put-ten-caps-in-me fucked.

Not a pretty image.

"Listen. I don't have time to explain everything to you right now. But we may be in some very deep shit. And I have a very bad feeling. I need you to answer me a question." I thumbed through my rolodex of people who might be a chink in the armor, who knew Marco's inner circle even more than *I* did. "Let's see...who brought you here?"

Louisa's cute hazel eyes looked very worried all of a sudden.

"One of Marco's guys drove me in. Sapo, I think."

"Did you chat with Sapo on the way here? Did he say anything at all?"

She twirled her hair with her index finger.

"Um, yeah, I think he said something about how he needed me to distract you."

"Distract me? From what?" That could mean so many different things.

"Or trade me for something? Maybe it was someone. I don't know what he said exactly, his accent is so thick."

I grabbed her shoulders.

"Louisa. I need specifics. Clues. Hints. Names!"

"Um well. He kept talking about some girl and laughing. I think he said her name was Eva?"

My hair stood on end. "Did you say *Eva?*"

"Yeah, definitely Eva. Why?"

Well then. The jig was fucking up. I felt like I'd just had the wind knocked out of me.

I heard a loud bang and voices outside the door. *That is not a knock. That is a gun.*

"Holy fuck," I growled.

I locked the door to the bathroom. It wouldn't hold them forever, but it would at least serve the function of slowing them down.

"What are you doing? What's going on?" she screeched. We both heard several hard blows on the door outside leading into the room. I reached the obvious conclusion:

Marco knew Eva was not Alexa, he knew about the chip in the rubik's cube, but he wanted to screw with us before he killed us.

And not just *figuratively screw*. Well, Eva at least.

I ripped out the towel rack and used it to shatter the bathroom window that led to the outside balcony. I jumped up into the window frame.

I might not have been Louisa's biggest fan, but it wasn't her fault she got mixed up in all this.

"Take my hand goddamn it, just do it."

"I'm scared, though," she said.

"Take it!"

She reluctantly grabbed hold of my hand and I pulled her up onto the frame of the window. Now that we were both outside, I pulled myself up onto the roof, and she followed. Or to be more accurate I pulled her up almost entirely. The girl seemed scared shitless.

Once we were on top of the roof, the sun shone down on the vast property.

"Do exactly as I say, and we *might* make it out of this alive," I said.

"Okay," she said, sniffling.

We ran across the roof and I heard Marco's guys climb up onto the balcony, yelling in our general direction. We scrambled over to a ladder and up another level, barely out of their sight. They hadn't seen us, but they'd find us soon undoubtedly.

We sat with our backs against the brick wall. Gunshots echoed through the air, and Louisa trembled.

"I'm scared, Corbin."

"I know. And it's not your fault you're involved in all of this—it's mine. So wait here. If they come near you, you've got this." I handed her the bar from the towel rack.

"You're not going to leave me, are you?" she asked, teary eyed.

"There's only one way I can stop them. And it's not by staying here."

I popped my eyes over the roof and assessed the situation. There were three of those fuckers, they all had assault rifles, and they were headed our way. It was about a fifteen foot drop down from our level to where the thugs were coming toward us.

"Louisa, you're a good woman. I don't care what Marco says about you. Wait here--and I'll be back."

She nodded, scrunched against the roof.

Like me, she knew there was only one way out of this.

I took a twenty foot running start and jumped, aiming for their little black haired heads before they even looked up.

31

EVA

My hands were tied behind my back in a chair in Marco's bedroom. So what if Marco knew I was named Eva? Maybe the audio just picked that up. I was hopeful.

Although this situation was looking more dire by the minute.

"I heard Corbin calling you Eva," Marco said, speaking slowly. "So I did a little research. Turns out you work for the DEA. Imagine that."

Well, there went that idea. *I'm screwed. And not in the way Corbin screws.*

Marco's phone buzzed, and he answered it. "Yes?...No!...Unacceptable!...Well FIND THEM. How hard is it to find the only tall white guy on MY OWN FUCKING PROPERTY?!"

He hung up his cell phone and dropped it with a thud on his desk. "Bunch of fucking clowns I have working for me," he mumbled.

I sat up, arched my back and stuck out my chest. "So this

is it, huh. Why don't you just kill me and get it over with. If you're going to kill me, might as well."

Marco picked up the gun off his desk and stuffed it in his waistband. "I'm still deciding what to do with you, *mi amor*. I might just lock you up and throw you in a dungeon for a few years. DEA agent with a pretty face like yours? You'd make the ultimate bargaining piece. It'd be all over the news. You'd make a great insurance policy if they ever caught Luis."

I stifled a shudder. Desperate times called for desperate measures. Marco had a chink in his armor, and damned if I didn't at least try to exploit it: his Kanye West-sized ego.

"You know Marco, I always did find you...the most attractive out of everyone here. I mean between you and Corbin...it's really no contest. You're powerful."

He took a few steps toward me and squatted down so we were at eye level, careful to make sure I could see his gun. "Do not bullshit a bullshitter, *mi amor*."

"You think I'm bullshitting? Try me. I want you, Marco," I said.

I saw it in his eyes. He was faltering. He stole a glance at the scoop neck I was wearing and gave the international guy 'I'm dazed and staring at your cleavage' look.

"I always have," I continued. "I don't care about the DEA. You think I would take on this mission if I thought I would come out alive? I wanted to get close to you. Corbin though—he wouldn't let me out of his sight. He's too worried about ruining his chance to get that time off his sentence."

He pulled out his gun and ran the cold metal of the nozzle down my face.

"You couldn't handle me," Marco said with a sadistic smile.

"Please, honey," I said, my lips parting. I squinted. "I'm a freak, just like you."

Marco's jaw dropped, and for a few moments I actually had him speechless.

"Oh, I get it now. It makes sense. You're not the boss. You're not the one who gets to decide my fate. You're waiting for Luis, since he's finally coming in this afternoon."

He put his hands on his stomach and let out a big belly laugh. "Oh, you're good. You're really good. I can see why Corbin would fall in love with you."

"...Fall in love with me?"

"Like I said, stop playing coy, Eva. The jig is up. I've been listening and watching you and Corbin since you got here. It's been quite entertaining for me—like reality TV with some hot sex."

"You mean, you're not just going to pass me off to Luis Reyes?"

"Bitch," he said in a low tone, his voice suddenly more menacing. "I *am* Luis Reyes."

A chill ran from my head to the tip of my toes.

"I...I don't believe you," I said.

He picked up the rubik's cube from the desk and turned it a few more times.

"Do you know what a figurehead is?"

"Of course, it's like the president of the United States. Everyone thinks he's a big deal but he really has no control over everything."

"Exactly. Why would the most powerful man of the most powerful cartel want to be a figurehead? That's not a fun life."

"So...Luis Reyes is a figurehead? I don't get it."

"Luis Reyes is a figment of the imagination. A brilliant fucking idea I had years ago. I wanted to keep the feds off my track, because who comes after a low level cocaine dealer when you can go after his boss, one of the biggest drug dealers on the face of the earth? So I invented Luis Reyes as the head of this organization." He made quotes around "Luis Reyes" as he said the words.

"So the DEA has been chasing a ghost for years? Wow."

"Impressed?" he smiled brutally.

"I mean, that's sort of brilliant. And it also really pisses me off that I didn't figure this out. "You're...Luis Reyes. Sort of. Shit. Why didn't I see that!"

Marco half scowled, half smiled. "Now you're getting it. Ah! Look at that!" he spun the rubik's cube once more and solved it. "Too bad you and Corbin couldn't solve this puzzle as fast as I did."

I tried to hold a seductive smile, but it was getting harder with every passing second. A feeling of regret and of courage, and of pure emotion welled up in me. "Like I said. If you're going to kill me, just get it over with. Do it. Like a man."

"Nah, I have a better idea."

"What's that?"

"Do you like it rough?" Marco said with a scowl.

Before I had a chance to hit him back, Marco hit me with the butt of the gun and everything went black.

32

CORBIN

T wo of the men turned toward me just soon enough to take a leg each to the head. Their bodies crunched as they hit the roof.

Dumb fucks. Their bodies made a nice soft landing pad and I rolled onto the roof. If they weren't dead, they were close to it.

The third man tried to point his gun at me, but I grabbed it and headbutted him before he had a chance to take aim. I picked up both of their AK-47s and took off running across the rest of the roof.

I was a little surprised Marco had his men after me and didn't kill me himself. This seemed like something that Marco would want to do personally—he always was very personal when it came to settling his debts. He always wanted to know all of the details, all of the ins and outs of the deals we would do. He was Luis Reyes' right hand man.

I got down on my belly and peered over the roof into the courtyard. The building was square shaped with an open air courtyard in the middle, typical of beautiful Mexican architecture. They really knew how to make beautiful shit here.

Eva crossed my mind. She was the epitome of an American beauty. What had she called it? "Mirish?" It was hard to smile when I knew she was in Marco's possession. I should never have let her out of my sight. *Either way, she doesn't love you, jackass. She made that crystal clear.*

I was man enough to admit that I'd always been a selfish asshole, for as long as I could remember. I'd been with girls for my own benefit. It was funny, but even before I knew Eva was just using me for her little one night stand—she was the exception. I wanted to give her everything. Yeah I pictured her sexy ass in a short skirt spread against the wall, but I wanted more with her. Even in a life or death situation, I pictured she and I getting a place together, me getting an honest job, And now, even though I knew she wasn't in love with me, I still felt that way.

I closed my eyes and shook it off. I was sweating balls and had a fucking mission that required my complete concentration. I opened my eyes and planned my attack. From my position, I could see two thugs walking around on the bottom level with AK's. If I came in their range, I was dead. On the Second level was the same thing. I felt like I was in the middle of a James Bond movie.

Think, you motherfucker.

The guy on the second floor patio was swatting flies and he wandered within striking distance. I swung down from the roof legs first and dropped right onto him, covering his mouth with my hand and wrapping my legs around his neck. He struggled for a moment until I twisted, and felt the crack of his neck as it spun. His body went limp and I broke his fall on the way down. I opened the door to the nearest room and dragged his body inside.

It took a couple of minutes to get his clothes and gear off of him, but I emerged from the room with his red shirt, jeans, sunglasses, and an AK-47 strapped across my stomach, looking just like him. Except, you know, for the fact that I was a foot taller than him, brown haired and blue eyed. And his pants were tight as hell. At a first glance though, a fellow guard might hesitate, and that would be all I'd need.

I went back outside to the balcony, meandering slowly to the other side where I saw another guy walking along the same balcony. He saw me but looked to be too focused on watching the courtyard downstairs to think I could actually be the guy that everyone was trying to kill. He kept glancing at a particular door—which I assumed would be Marco's room. I needed to know for sure, though. I only had one chance at finding the spot where Marco, and by my logic, Eva was as well.

I racked my brain for a way to determine if Marco was in there. After a few seconds, I opted for the easiest route. In a flawless Spanish accent, I asked, "Is the boss in there?"

"Sí," he responded.

Well that was easy.

"Thank you," I said as I kneed him straight in the balls and punched him in the face so hard he went limp and hit the ground.

Damn, I still had it.

I rolled my sleeves up and knocked on the door. "Jefe," I boomed, my accent harkening back to my days in Chula Vista when people were shocked that a white boy could speak Spanish so well. "Open the door, please. We need to talk."

I crouched down, with good fucking reason because the next thing I knew the door was blown to bits with bullets at chest and head height. I considered returning fire, but I couldn't expose myself.

"Go out there and see who you killed," I heard Marco's voice.

A man poked his head out of the hole in the door, looked down and saw me. His eyes went wide. Before he could react, I yanked him out of the door and threw him over the balcony into the courtyard.

I opened the door, yanking it off the handle since it was already destroyed. I dove inside and saw my own personal nightmare. Eva was slumped over on a chair with a huge red mark on her head. Marco pointed his gun at my head.

"It's all over, Corbin," he said. "In less than a minute my men will be coming through that door, you'll be outnumbered, and I'll have you shot. You and the bitch." His eyes darted to Eva.

I didn't yell or scream, as much as I wanted to. Marco's momentary lapse in attention allowed me to take a quick step toward him. I punched him dead in the face.

The first blow connected, and I knocked the gun out of his hand. He fell to the ground, grasping for his weapon, and I jumped on top of him. I held his shirt in my hand, delivering blow after blow. I was ready to pound him again, but heard a shot and looked up. Four of Marco's henchmen stood with guns in hand, all pointed at me.

"Let go of the boss," one of them said. "It's over."

With no choice, I dropped Marco's unconscious, limp body to the ground, and stood up. My hands were sweaty and bloody along with my shirt.

"He's alive," one said, taking Marco's pulse.

"Could have fooled me," I growled.

"What do we do, take him dead or alive?"

"Marco said shoot to kill if necessary."

I looked at the whites of the men's eyes. As fucked up as it was, I didn't care if they killed me. I had killed, and many would say I deserved to die. But what I couldn't deal with was Eva going through any more pain. I could see her chest barely rising and falling in her chair.

"Let's take the woman first," the fourth chimed in. The other three smiled and looked toward him in agreement. Sick fucks.

"The hell you will. You're going through me first. Why don't you put the gun down and fight like men."

They looked down at Marco's bloody body I had almost destroyed in under a minute. They knew hand to hand combat with me was basically a death sentence for them.

"Let's just shoot the woman and then have our way with her," one of them said.

My blood curdled as I stood between them and Eva. "You want her? You're going to have to pry her away from my cold, lifeless fingers."

The thugs hesitated, deciding what to do.

I stood in front of her. "Well boys, go ahead, do it. Do your fucking duty you thugs."

I heard gunshots in the distance, and one of the men turned. I saw one of their bodies fall down to the ground. Another one of them turned toward me, aimed, and fired at me.

Instantaneously I felt an impact on my chest and my vision went blurry. The last thing I remembered was Eva's scent before everything went dark.

33

EVA

"Eva. Eva!" a voice yelled. Cold water hit my face and I opened my eyes.

Ned stood before me holding an empty cup. "Oh my God, Eva, you're alive!" he hugged me.

"A little help?" My eyes darted to my hands, still tied behind my back..

"Oh, sorry, I didn't even see that."

The three dead bodies of Marco's assassins laid in various parts of the room, bloody. Ned untied me, and I tried to stand up.

I refocused my eyes to make sure I wasn't dreaming. It really was him.

"Ned? How did you get here? What the hell happened?" I tried to focus my eyes on Ned but I couldn't. Woozy, I sat back down.

"This little guy came in handy," Ned said, tossing the solved rubik's cube up in the air. "We had been listening to Marco for two whole weeks. We waited until just the right moment—when Marco finally confessed to you that there *was no* Luis Reyes, and then we moved in."

"Just the right moment? What the hell is the matter with you? Our lives were in danger! Where is Corbin?! Is he dead?" My heart beat fast, but I still couldn't stand.

Ned looked down. "Corbin's not with us."

"Not with us? What the hell does that mean?" Tears streamed down my cheeks.

Ned pursed his lips like a priest searching for the right words. Extending an arm, he put a hand on my shoulder. "Corbin took several bullets to his body. It doesn't look like he'll make it."

"Is he going to be okay?"

Ned said nothing and turned away from me.

Of course it would happen like this. The moment I decided that I loved a man, he was taken from me. The past couple of weeks in the Reyes mansion flashed through my mind like a cheesy movie montage of cuddling, screwing, and witty banter. The tears came harder at the thought of never seeing Corbin again.

"Here's some water," Ned said, handing me a bottle. "You're probably dehydrated." He rubbed my back.

I took a drink, put my head in my hands and let out a parade of tears.

"Thank God Corbin was just a criminal," Ned says. "I'd hate to have to report an agent death to headquarters."

I swallowed hard, and my tears turned to anger. "Excuse me?"

Ned paced slowly around the room. "Corbin was a criminal. He was a bad person. And you know what else? Seeing you in danger has really made me think. About *us.*"

I actually spewed out the water that I was drinking. I stood up, fury replacing my lightheadedness. "About *us*? You've got to be fucking kidding me right now."

Ned scrunched his brow at the F-bomb I dropped. He

thought I was a damn angel. "Kidding you? No, Eva, I really neglected you, and driving you to...you know. Knowing that you were so close to danger really made me think—"

"Don't think," I actually slapped Ned hard on his cheek. "Where is Corbin? Take me to him. *Now*."

Ned held his cheek in utter shock.

"He's in a helicopter, about to be evacuated." Ned pointed out the door.

"Where are you going?" Ned shouted as I grazed him on the way out of the room.

"I'm going to find Corbin. I'm fucking in love with him. And you, sir, are an asshole."

Ned's jaw hung open. He was used to *nice* Eva. *Never raise her voice* Eva. Well, *nice* Eva is gone. I felt more Alexa than Eva, and Alexa knew how to be firm, forward, and—when necessary—downright bitchy if I didn't get what I wanted.

In the distance, I heard a helicopter. I didn't walk. I ran. I sprinted. I took off my heels and threw them away. My dress was dirty with sweat and blood stains and I couldn't care less.

I saw swaths of DEA and FBI agents and more helicopters throughout the Reyes property. Marco's assassins and guards were held in handcuffs on the ground. There was no sign of Marco. That mustached motherfucker probably got away. Whatever.

"Where is Corbin?" I screamed at one of the guards. He pointed toward a helicopter with its blades already spinning, about to take off. Arriving before it could lift off, I pounded on the door until the medic inside opened it. Corbin was lying on a cot with his arms on his side, as pale as a corpse. It was loud as hell from the helicopter spinning its blade so I grabbed one of the microphone headsets to speak into.

"Is Corbin okay?" I asked.

"He suffered four shots, one to the stomach and three to the back and shoulder. I don't think he's going to make it. And sorry, lady, you can't be in here."

Giving the medic a nasty look for calling me 'lady,' I put a headset over Corbin's ears and spoke into the helicopter's microphone. "Corbin, baby. I love you. I fucking love you. I don't know what this was the last two weeks. I have no idea how this happened. But I love you and you're going to stay alive. You hear me?"

Corbin's eyes opened just a smidge. I leaned down and kissed him on the lips. Another tear rolled down my cheek.

"Thanks...Alexa," he says slowly. I swore I saw him crack the tiniest smile.

Even when he was on the brink of death he screwed with me. Sonofabitch.

"Who's Alexa? I thought you were Eva Napleton? Are you authorized to be here?" one of the helicopter techs said to me.

I shook my head. "Long story."

"Listen," the tech went on. "This is really touching and all, but we've got to fly to San Diego right freaking now to get him to a hospital. And we need to fly as light as possible."

"I'm not leaving him," I said

The two of them looked at each other. "Alright, fuck it," the pilot said. "Prepare for takeoff."

We lifted off the ground, and I saw the landscape surrounding Marco's beautiful mansion disappear in the distance behind us.

I took Corbin's hand in my own and said a silent prayer.

34

EVA

"I'm sorry ma'am, you won't be able to see Mr. Young. It's family only." A nurse stood in front of me with a clipboard and a drowsy face. It looked like she'd been working all night.

"It's fine, I'm his partner," I argued.

She narrowed her eyes and spoke in an unempathetic tone. "Are you married?"

"Not exactly," I said. "We're undercover agent partners. Now please, let me through."

"Really? *You're* an undercover agent?" She scoffed, giving me an up-and-down. I could see where she was coming from. My red dress was smudged with sweat—and even some blood.

How could I explain what was going on to this woman in words that she would understand?

Someone said something to her on the walkie-talkie on her hip, and she turned her head. "You need where? Okay."

She put her hand on my arm. "Please excuse me, Miss. Your partner should be in surgery for another five hours. I suggest you get some rest and clean yourself up. Need to be clean in front of the patients, you know."

With that, she turned and walked through the automatic double doors into the rest of the hospital. The doors closed abruptly in my face.

Frustrated, I walked over to the seats in the waiting room and fired off a text to Amanda. I shut my eyes.

~

"If I didn't know any better, I'd think you were a homeless person," I heard Amanda's voice and felt her hand on my shoulder. I opened my sleepy lids and looked down at my body, which was covered in sweat and dirt. I could see how she might get that impression.

"Long story," I groaned.

"I'd love to hear it. Here, put this on. It'll help you look a little less homeless at least." She handed me a cardigan. It wasn't really my style, but I decided now was not the time to worry about having a fashionable appearance. I took it and put it on.

"What time is it?" I asked groggily.

"It's almost midnight."

"Oh my gosh, Corbin is out of surgery!" I sat up with a sudden surge of adrenaline.

"Okay, stop," she said, sitting down next to me. "You have some explaining to do. First, you go off the grid for two straight weeks. I know you said you were on vacation, but you didn't return a single text or send me any 'lol's at the funny email links I sent you. What the hell? That's not normal for you."

I took a deep breath. Fuck it. The only good news I'd gotten if I was being honest was Marco's death--which would probably be all over the news soon, anyway. "Can you keep a secret?"

"Are you really asking *me* if I can keep a secret? I'm a lawyer. And your best friend. I'm offended."

I rubbed my face. "It's just...it's classified. But I'll tell you. Remember how I was talking about Corbin and I going undercover together? Well we did. I was undercover as Corbin's mistress."

If Amanda's jaw dropped any further, it would be on the floor.

"Corbin's...*mistress?*"

"I love you Amanda, but I'm too tired to fill in all of the blanks. The long short of it is Corbin's in surgery now and they don't know if he's going to make it."

My heart dropped just thinking about Corbin not making it. The dam broke and I began to cry. Amanda hugged me.

"I'm sorry to hear that," she said. "You...really care about Corbin now, don't you. I thought he was just a one night stand?"

I forced a smile to combat my tears. I had no idea how to describe what there was between Corbin and I, even to my best friend.

"It's okay," she said, recognizing my discomfort. She wrapped me up in a tight, warm hug. "We don't have to talk about it now."

We were interrupted by the sound of the big automatic double doors in the waiting room opening. The same nurse from before walked out.

"Miss Napleton?" she said, looking at her clipboard.

"Yes?" I strode toward her eagerly.

"I have news about Corbin. Maybe you want to sit back down for this."

"Okay...but is he going to make it?"

"We're not sure."

This was a low point. I had finally let myself go with a man—and he loved me back—but he was going to die.

It felt like the walls were caving in around me.

35

CORBIN

I woke up and saw a bright white light.

Maybe I'd died and gone to heaven.

But I remembered how I hadn't exactly been a gleaming example of a well-behaved man who would end up in St. Peter's good graces.

It was more likely that I was back in solitary confinement where they left the lights on for 24 hours to fuck with me. *My own personal hell.*

The bright light disappeared, and I sensed her. I smelled her. She was there.

I opened my eyes. And saw Eva sitting next to me. Her eyes were tired, her clothes were dirty except for the sweater she had on, and her brown eyes had never looked sexier.

"Oh my God Corbin, you're alive!" she gasped.

"Hey," I mustered, and when I said the words my chest hurt like hell. "Where am I?"

She took my hand in hers. "We're at Scripps Mercy. Back in San Diego."

"How did we get to San D...oh my God that hurts." My entire chest cavity ached like a freight train had run over it.

"You were shot. Four times. Do you remember? They almost didn't let me in to see you."

"Jesus." I looked down at my chest and saw a white bandage covering me. I groaned. I remembered the first shot, but I wasn't sure how many I took after that.

We sat in silence, words unnecessary for a moment. Eva smiled softly and ran her fingers along the ridges of my palms. I'd never been comfortable with that kind of tender touching—recoiled at it even—but with Eva, it made my heart tingle.

"Did we catch Marco?"

"We did. We took him out. Thanks to you. You almost sacrificed your life for mine," she whispered, her hand still gently touching mine.

A doctor walked in, ending our moment.

"Corbin, I'm Doctor Peterson. You are one lucky man," the doctor said, putting up some X-rays against a board. I tried to turn my head, but moving was hard, so I decided to just close my eyes and enjoy Eva's touch.

"Well, either lucky or tough," the doctor went on. "You were shot four times. but the shots missed all of your vital organs. Give it a few more weeks and you—well, I was going to say you'll be good as new, but that's just not true. You'll have a few scars. But you'll live."

"By the way, who are you? Are you his wife?" the doctor said, turning to Eva. "Are you okay to be here?"

"It's okay," I murmured, opening my eyes and taking Eva's hand. "She's my mistress."

The doctor looked up from his clipboard with a funny expression. Eva saw where I was going and played along instantly, running her hand up and down my leg.

"Yeah, he needs a little...special medicinal technique that I know," she said, rubbing my leg.

I smiled and that's all I could do, because it hurt to laugh.

The doctor shrugged. "Well, uh, I guess you can be here even though you're not family if the patient is okay with it. Just as long as this medicinal technique isn't unauthorized." He nodded and glanced at his clipboard again. "I'll check back up on you tomorrow. Have a good night you two."

Just like that we were alone again.

I smiled. We were alone again, and I wasn't dead and in hell. On the contrary, I was in heaven with Eva rubbing her hand on my leg, gradually creeping it further up. She had easy access to my bare thigh since all I was wearing was a gown and some briefs.

"What are you doing?" I asked. "I think you're getting close to my danger zone."

"Danger zone?" she smiled. "Is that what you're calling it now?"

"Eva...we're not playing anymore," I said.

"I'm not playing. I'm taking care of business. I need to see if something still works."

She slid her hand up my thigh and took me in her hand.

"Alexa...I mean Eva...sorry...fuck."

She looked up at me with the same beautiful brown eyes that had drawn me in that first night at the club.

"What did I do to deserve this?" I said.

"Corbin. I want to be yours. I want to be your Eva. Your Alexa. And everything in between."

"So you're saying you want to have really dirty sex and also be my trophy wife who cooks and cleans?"

"Shut up you silly boy," she smiled.

"Gotta keep the jokes up in a long term relationship, right?"

"I love you, Corbin," she said.

"I love you, too."

She worked her way down with her mouth and I decided this is the best medicine a man could have.

And no, I wasn't thinking about the work she was doing between my legs.

I was thinking about love.

Who has the dirty mind now?

EPILOGUE

10 Months Later

Eva

I sliced my way through the crowd until I found an open seat at the bar. I took it, drawing looks from both of the men on either side of me. I was dressed in high heels and a black scoop neck dress so tight I had to wiggle for a minute to fit into it, so I wasn't surprised that I was being ogled. The men tried to be sly when they stared at my curves by looking away the moment I glanced in their direction.

Nice try, boys. I smiled. *If you are going to look, just look.*

I ordered a tequila on the rocks with a lime. The man to my right leaned over and poked me on the arm.

"That's quite a drink for a lady," he said.

I smiled back and batted my eyes.

"Well I'm not your average lady." I put a hand on his as I took a sip of my drink. Putting the glass down, I lowered my voice and whispered in his ear. "I want to party. Can you help me?"

He raised his eyebrows in a surprised look. "You want...to *party?*"

"Yes. You understand what I mean, right?"

I put my finger to my nostril and sniffed; the universal symbol for needing to order the world's most expensive white powder.

"Why yes of course," he said. "Come with me."

I followed him down a stairwell and into a hall where the bathrooms were. The light dimmed and a wave of nervousness flowed through me as he opened a door with no window.

We were the only ones inside the bathroom. He shut the wooden door and locked it with a click.

"How much do you want?"

"A half pound."

He laughed. "You don't have that much money."

"You don't think so?" I said, and pulled out a wad of hundreds. He took the money from me and counted it. "Two thousand dollars is not nearly enough. But I think we can arrange something."

He snapped his fingers and two other men appeared from behind a secret door in the back of the bathroom.

"Jose, Manny, what do you think? This whore worth an extra three thousand?"

"I say we pay her a thousand for each of us."

"One thousand for each of you? What do you mean?" I scrunched my face in confusion. "Two thousand should be plenty."

Goddammit, why does this happen every time?

The men closed in on me from three different angles. The lock started rattling.

"This bathroom is occupied," the man fumed.

Even though I knew it was coming, I flinched as the

wooden door was literally ripped from its frame, and Corbin appeared.

"Who the fuck are you?" the main man asked Corbin.

Corbin saw the men touching me and let out an honest to God snarl.

I flinched again as he threw a punch so close to my face I felt the wind from Corbin's fist as he hit the first man, who fell into the toilet and stopped moving. Corbin spun around and hit another one of the attackers in the nose and the man fell limp into a heap on the ground.

I stood behind the third man, who pulled out a gun and pointed it.

"Stand down, asshole," he said, taking a step toward Corbin.

My heart thumping, I delivered a hard left hand chop to the man's neck, striking precisely the place I wanted at his Adam's apple. He reacted automatically, beginning to wheeze for air. I pounced on his arm and disarmed him of the gun. Corbin gave him a right hook to the nose and the man's body went down to the ground like a brick thrown in a river.

Corbin and I stood back to back, all three of the men out cold around us. He wiped the blood from his fist off on his pants.

"Baby, you okay?" I asked.

"It's not my blood," Corbin answered. "It's that dumbass's. I think." He raised his chin toward the guy whose head was in the toilet.

There was a loud bang on the bathroom door, and Ned entered with his gun drawn, followed by a S.W.A.T. team of ten men.

"Shit, looks like you guys took care of em' already. They dead?"

Ned ambled over to the man and took his pulse.

"Nah," Corbin answered. "Alive. I didn't hit him too hard. You might want to get him to a hospital, though."

Ned shook his head. "I gotta hand it to you, I never thought you two would play such a convincing couple. The bad boy and the good girl."

I rolled my eyes. "The good girl?"

"Yeah, of course," Ned responded. "You've always been the too nice girl, Eva."

I really needed to think of a way to tell Ned that what Corbin and I were doing wasn't an act anymore. I mean, it had been ten months since Corbin and I had started 'playing' work partner to take down a record number of criminals. I was surprised Ned hadn't figured it out yet himself, but he had the ability to be quite dense at times.

"Ned, I know when we were dating I was a good girl. You know, sex only missionary style in the dark and all that, but..."

Corbin scrunched his face and gave me a confused look, knowing I wasn't a big one for confessionals. After all the time we'd spent hanging out the past few months, I knew it took a lot to catch him off guard. And I loved doing it.

I continued. "Ned, there is something you need to know about me. All of that 'acting' I was doing with Corbin? Well..."

I walked over to Corbin with an authoritative strut.

No more little Miss Nice girl.

I pushed him into the wall, wrapped my leg around his waist and pulled his head down to mine for a wet, sloppy kiss. I grabbed his hand and placed it directly on the fabric of my dress that was barely covering my ass.

During our make out, I opened the corner of my eye and I could see Ned's mouth completely agape.

I released Corbin and turned to Ned.

"You're just gonna have to get used to the new me, Ned. And I'm not really a *nice* girl. I'm sorry. No actually, I'm sorry I'm not sorry."

Ned came down off his shock cloud and managed to say a few words.

"I thought I noticed something in your attitude, and well I guess..."

Corbin had his arm on my back, and it was slipping downward toward that spot just below the small of my back he always liked to grab. In the past four months I hadn't gone two days without having his big hands all over me.

"Well...?" I said, tapping my toe once.

"And whatever you're doing, you're catching the shit out of these criminals. We've busted more with you two under-cover in the past eight months than in the past four years. Shit, who am I to judge. Perez, Gatsburg, let's get these guys on cots and get them out of here." Ned signaled to his S.W.A.T. officers and they carried the criminals out. Corbin and I lingered.

"Alright," Ned said, "Good work here. As a reward, we're giving you a month off. Take a vacation. Do something that doesn't involve taking down drug dealers for a change. For the love of God, lay low. I need to give you two a break."

I nodded. Ned exited the bathroom, leaving Corbin and I alone.

"Damn, what are we gonna do for a month?" I said as the door clicked shut. I moved to follow Ned out, but Corbin grabbed my wrist and twirled me back toward him like I was doing a spin move on the dance floor. I hit his chest and he wrapped me up with his arms.

"I can think of a couple of things," he said with the trademark sparkle in his eye. He clicked the lock on the bathroom door shut. I smiled and gripped his shirt, tugging it upward in a not so subtle 'take it off' signal. He unbuttoned it and I ran my hands over his chest.

Nothing is hotter than a man with scars that he got saving your life.

I thought back to the pep talk I gave myself that changed it all, and I smiled.

No more Miss Nice girl.

Now it was more like Miss Bad girl. And I couldn't be happier. I ran my hand along his muscular leg, and accidentally scraped the outline of his jean's pocket and felt something hard and tiny inside.

"Hey," Corbin grabbed my wrist before I could wrap my hand around whatever it was. "You really have turned into a bad girl, haven't you."

"What is that in your pocket? I must know!" I laughed.

Corbin had a look on his face that I'd literally never seen him have before. He looked...nervous and shaky.

Suddenly I was confused.

"Well, fuck," Corbin said. "I wanted this to be a surprise, but..fuck it."

Corbin got down on one knee and pulled a ring out of his pocket.

"Eva Napleton, I love you. I love you as Eva and Alexa. I want all of your craziness for the rest of my life. No, take that back, I don't want it. I *need* it. Will you upgrade from being my fake mistress and real girlfriend to my wife?"

I looked down in amazement at the man kneeled in front of me. Old me would be pissed that this moment was so totally imperfect, that it was taking place in a bathroom, and that Corbin basically started this whole proposal with the words *fuck it.*

But the new me understood that the perfect moment

never came, except when you weren't looking for it. And in a weird way, this imperfect, tattooed, scarred young man was perfect for me.

"Get up here." I said, needing Corbin to not be kneeling, needing his arms wrapped around me.

Corbin stood up and slipped the ring on my finger. It was huge. He ran a hand through my hair and gave me an especially tender kiss. I made a mental note to figure out how Corbin got the money for this. I was guessing it wasn't from the meager government salary the DEA paid us. For now, I'd let it go.

The tender kiss led to tonsil hockey, which led our hands all over each other and eventually to my dress coming off over my head.

I sat on the sink and arched my back feeling Corbin's hard, sweaty body against mine, and a peculiarly naughty thought crossed my mind:

Best one night stand ever. I couldn't wait to have a one night stand with Corbin every night for the rest of my life.

ACKNOWLEDGMENTS

There is even more of a story behind this book then I've talked about yet.

The book that is now Dirty Trick is the first book I ever tried to write. I put this one on the shelf a long time ago. I was pretty self critical when I started out.

Sure, I went back and edited the shit out of it, added in some key scenes, and solicited a ton of feedback from my amazing Beta readers and friends.

But the heart and soul of this book is an idea I had about three years ago--an idea I refused to give up on.

I am already hearing some readers saying things like "favorite Mickey Miller book ever," "this is different then your *normal* books," and "strongest female lead you've written, well done."

So I want to say thank you, thank you, thank you to everyone for being along with me on this journey. It's sure been an amazing ride since I started about a year and a half ago and decided to write openly as a man who writes (and loves writing) romance. Also I hope this little story will serve the budding writers out there who are reading this! You're a lot more creative and powerful then you think you are, trust me on this.

And if you're reading this during release week, I'm doing a giveaway for 10 signed paperbacks in my Facebook Group, Mickey's Misfits. Just search 'Mickey's Misfits' on Facebook to find us!

Thanks to everyone who has believed in me and this book with their ever positive attitudes and vibes. Virginie, Dani, Megan, Barb, Becky, Sara, Dan E., Will M. and many more. And also Carly B. who gave me the crash course at the beginning of my career that I needed.

Thanks so much for reading and love you guys! Enjoy the Bonus Novel!

ALSO BY MICKEY MILLER:

Blackwell After Dark - Small Town Romances

Also By Mickey Miller:

Ballers Romance Series:

Standalones:

Also By Mickey Miller:

Mickey Miller books cowritten with Holly Dodd:

Dirty CEO

Hotblooded Prizefighter

Made in the USA
Lexington, KY
20 August 2018